Murder by E-mail

Jim Kilpatrick

PublishAmerica
Baltimore

© 2005 by Jim Kilpatrick
All rights reserved. No part of this book may be reproduced, stored in a retrieval system or transmitted in any form or by any means without the prior written permission of the publishers, except by a reviewer who may quote brief passages in a review to be printed in a newspaper, magazine or journal.

First printing

ISBN: 1-4137-7571-3
PUBLISHED BY PUBLISHAMERICA, LLLP
www.publishamerica.com
Baltimore

Printed in the United States of America

*For Richard Ringgold, a true friend and buddy.
Thanks, guy*

Lt. James (Jimmy) Hong sat behind his desk reading the morning paper, his usual mug of coffee locked in his hand on the chair arm. He was scanning the front page looking to see what the press had discovered about the last two murders on Oahu. It seemed they always knew the answers before the police did, or at least they tried to present the idea that they did. Hong was a thirty-year man on the force and well respected by everyone. He had broken the several cases that had been tossed in the "unsolvable" files. He was noted for his silence when he worked on a case and wildness when he was off duty. He had lost his wife ten years ago when she was killed in a hit-and-run automobile accident on the Pali Highway. Since then he had visited her grave every day when his shift ended, sometimes spending hours sitting on the grass beside her tombstone, talking softly to her.

He turned the page and continued to read.

Across from him sat Sgt. Connie Jones. An eleven-year vet of the force, she had made detective in just three years. A rapid rise for anyone in the police field, she had helped Hong find the murderer of his wife in just six months, while only a beat officer. CJ, as she preferred to be called, was married with three children. Her husband, Rick, was a police officer when they met seven years ago, but had left the force due to an injury. It had been love at first sight. They had married one year later and the first of the children followed one year after. Rick was the apple of CJ's world and of course the children were the apples of both their lives.

CJ stared at the blank piece of paper on his desk. Every lead so far on the killings of the two women had been a dead end. The murdered women didn't know each other, didn't work in the same part of town, and didn't have any friends in common. The only things in common were that both were between thirty-five and forty years old, lived alone, had nice homes, were nude when found, nothing was stolen, and they were murdered in their living rooms.

There appeared to be no motive for either murder, yet according to Hong, they were tied together somehow. For the first time since becoming a detective, Jones was lost. She looked up as Hong rustled the newspaper.

"You know CJ, we are missing something, something right in front of us. We should be able to see it, but we don't. I know the crime lab went over the scenes with a fine tooth comb, but damn it, either we missed something or they did."

"I agree, but what?"

Hong only shook his head and laid the newspaper on the desk. He reached into the desk drawer and retrieved a folder packed with photos. Opening it, he spread the photos on the newspaper and desk. Jones came around and peered over his shoulder at the mass of photos of the dead body and room where it lay. Nothing was overturned, nothing amiss. It was like the murderer had cleaned up the room, dusted, swept and placed everything back where it had been before the crime.

It was right there in front of them but they couldn't see it. There was some little item that they had over looked. It was the average dining room: table, four chairs, white tablecloth, even dishes laid out for the next meal; pictures on the walls, a sliding door to the lanai; and over in one corner, a computer with printer and scanner. Something you would see in just about every house on the islands, but something was there that they had overlooked, something that would take them to the murderer.

"I don't see anything different than before, boss!"

"Nor do I CJ, but I guarantee it's there."

They continued to stare at the photos looking for the missing clue, when Captain Streeter cleared his throat and they looked up.

"Anything new?"

"Nothing right now, but I'm sure it's there, somewhere in these photos. Something we missed."

"Want any more to help on the detail?"

"No, CJ and I will figure it out. It will just take time."

"They all do; they all do," he said, walking away.

They went back to studying the photos. They scanned the room and checked for any small detail they might have missed. Finally CJ sat down disgusted.

"If it is there I don't see it."

"Then let's go look at it in person; maybe something will jump out at us there, that we are not seeing here in the photos."

Jones nodded. They strapped on their revolvers and tossed on light jackets to conceal their weapons and headed out to the parking lot for a vehicle. She always drove so Hong could do his thinking. He said he always thought better while cruising, as long as he wasn't doing the driving.

The drive to Hawaii Kai was about a half-hour, because of the traffic. When they arrived at the scene, the yellow ribbon was still up prohibiting anyone from entering the house without a police escort. The door was locked and Hong used his key to get in. It was a nice two-bedroom house with a small back yard. The house was spotless; the floors were waxed and shining. Every nook and cranny was dust free.

Hong walked over to the chalk outline on the floor, knelt, and placed his hand inside it, like he was drawing information from the remaining energy of the departed body. He closed his eyes and got flashes of light and forms in his mind's eye. It always happened to him. He could always feel something no one else could. This time, however, he wasn't able to get a clear picture, only bits and pieces, and nothing he could put a finger on.

This was all that remained of Lita Jackson, 37, single, blonde, blue-eyed, slim-figured, and very well-to-do in business. Jackson was like the other victim, Mary Wright, 39, single, brown-haired, green-eyed, slim-figured and on the rise in her company as well, yet neither of them knew the other.

Hong lingered by the chalk outline, rubbing his fingers on the floor.

"What do you think, boss?" Jones asked.

"I still don't know, but it's here right in front of us."

They walked around the room looking at everything, yet nothing clicked in their minds.

They were about to leave when Hong's eyes fell on the computer sitting next to the patio door. He walked to it and ran his fingers over the keys. Again flashes of light and misty figures came to his mind. He quickly pulled his hand away from the keyboard; sweat began to appear on his brow. He was staring at the screen like it was on and he had seen something on it.

"This is it, CJ. It's right here. It's in the computer; I can feel it. Was there a computer in Wright's home?"

"Yes, I think so. I can check it out."

"Do it!"

"There is a clue in each one of the computers. That's the something we over looked. Come on, let's go back to the office. There is still plenty to do before we find our killer."

The ride back to headquarters was as long as the drive out to Hawaii Kai, but when they arrived, the photos from the Wright house were sitting on Hong's desk, along with a report giving all the items in the dining room in detail. Near the top was one computer.

Hong had it impounded and sent to the evidence room. He would check it later, but inside he knew he had found the missing clues. The problem was what were the hidden clues in the computers? What would each machine tell him and how would it unlock the murder of the two women?

~~~

John Morris was busy at his desk at the Hawaiian Import/Export Company. He had spent most of the day working on a major speech he would be making to the Downtown Business Association. His secretary had spent most of the day doing rewrites as he changed first a word here and then a word there. He was reading the sixth copy of the speech with intensity. Being a perfectionist was at times good, and at times bad. He flipped on the intercom.

"Miss Puanani, would you come in here please?"

"Yes sir," came the tired reply.

"It looks good. Just set it in a more readable font and we can call it a day."

"Thank you sir. I'll have it ready in a few minutes."

"No. Call it a day. Just have it ready before noon tomorrow. Go home, Diane, and have a good night."

Diane Puanai was all smiles as she left Morris's office. It was actually early and she didn't often get to leave early in the day. She quickly cleaned off her desk and placed the to-be-re–fonted paper in the center with a post-it note reading, "do first thing." She was about to leave when Mrs. Morris came into the office.

"Good afternoon, Mrs. Morris. Mr. Morris just finished his speech for tomorrow. Please go on in."

Mrs. Morris only glanced at the lovely Hawaiian lady as she passed her.

Mrs. Morris had once been a model for a major agency in New York but now only worked when and where she liked, demanding a huge salary for even a minor shoot. She had met and married John when he had been in New York for a business meeting. Her fiery red hair and black eyes along with the knock down figure was more than Mr. Morris was able to withstand. In a whirlwind romance, with full press coverage, he wined and dined her from New York to Los Angeles, using the corporate jet. They were married in a week and then honeymooned in Europe for a month. It was one of those perfect marriages, the kind of marriages made in a Hollywood movie. He was the super athletic looking executive and she was the beautiful model with brains included.

"Hello, Amy dear. How was your day?"

"Hi honey. It was okay. You want to take me home? I have a big surprise for you tonight."

She pulled out a sexy black, silk nightgown, draping it on her shoulder and twirling around. Her eyes locked onto his. The silky gown attached itself to every curve on her body. She glided over to him, pushed him back his chair and straddled him. Her lips found his and they kissed deeply, passionately. She lifted the front of her skirt and reached between her legs and unzipped his pants, never releasing him from her kiss until he was ready for her. She broke the kiss and moaned softly.

"I'm not wearing any panties dear, and I need you right now."

He responded and they made love in his office chair. Finally they collapsed into each other's arms, smiling at each other. She kissed him on the lips softly, rose, and straightened her dress. She turned, smiled, and walked toward the door.

"There's more of that available when you take me home, love."

He couldn't resist her sexual aggressiveness. Something about it made him as weak as a kitten and yet his desire had already begun to rage in his body to take her home and bed her.

"Let me finish one item and we can go," he said, with lust in his voice.

He quickly closed out his computer and cleared his desk of loose papers. He readjusted his pants and smiled at his wife. She responded by licking her lips and lifting the hem of her dress to reveal a luscious, creamy, tanned thigh. He took her by the arm and they left the building, heading home to Kailua.

Over the Pali Highway they sped, heading for their home in Lanikai. John knew how sexual Amy was and how her desires raged uncontrollably. She sat beside him, inching closer and letting her lust play out. He knew that night would be filled with lovemaking. It would be her desires that he would have to fulfill. Not that he didn't have his own desires, but there were times he was not up to her standards in bed. She often would express her disappointment at his performance and berate him the next morning. But he loved her.

~ ~ ~

Detectives Hong and Jones were in the property room examining the two computers that had been impounded. Hong ran his fingers over Mary Wright's keyboard and saw in his mind the same misty scenes he had seen in Jackson's. CJ was looking at him and watched his face strain under the emotions flowing into his body. She pulled Hong's hand away, breaking the connection.

"Are you all right?" she asked.

"Yes, I'm all right but it is stronger in this keyboard than in the other."

They went back to the squad room. Hong called the technical people and had them work on the computer hard drive memories.

"I want everything you can retrieve from both hard drives. Is that understood? Good. I want it back in 24 hours."

He hung up the phone and stared at the photos on his desk. Jones could see his mind working behind his dark brown eyes. She could feel the anger he had for the murderer and she knew he had set his mind on finding and bringing the individual to trial.

It was several minutes before Hong sat down in his chair.

"Jim, it's late; maybe we should call it a day and go home."

"You go home. The family will be waiting and you haven't seen them in two days. I'll just spend a little more time here and then head out myself."

"You promise you will?"

"Yes, I promise."

Jones nodded and left the station. Hong stayed and read the reports over again and then he left.

CJ's house, in Kaneohe, was filled with laugher when she arrived. Rick met her at the door and kissed her as if they had been separated for twenty years. The children danced around her, hugging her legs and making attempts to get her attention. Angela, the eldest, Joel the middle child, and Harley were like hungry sharks in their attempts to have their mother touch them or say a word to them.

Dinner was waiting and they sat down as a family. It was noisy, as everyone wanted Mother's undivided attention. She answered many questions about her day and passed out praise for each of their accomplishments. They finished dinner and all trooped into the kitchen to help with the dishes. Again CJ was the center of attraction for the three children. Rick washed the dishes, knowing his turn with CJ would come later, after the children went to bed. Dishes done, they all went into to the living room where everyone piled on the sofa to watch some TV.

Around nine, the youngest, Harley was sound asleep, and the other two were headed in the same direction. Rick picked up Harley and carried her to her bedroom. Angela guided herself down the hallway to her bed and Joel was led by CJ to his room. After kissing each of them good night, CJ and Rick stood in Angela's doorway and cuddled against each other and smiled.

"We've got great kids," Rick said with a smile

"Yes, no doubt about it."

Rick closed the door and they walked back to the living room and sat down on the sofa. CJ curled up on his shoulder and closed her eyes.

"Tough day, honey?"

"Yes and we are not getting anywhere with the case. All the leads have dried up, but Jim thinks he has found something and you know him and his hunches. He is very seldom wrong."

"How was your day, dear?" CJ asked.

"Nothing much. Sold some cars and made a buck. That covers it. You tired?"

"Yes but never too tired for you," she said as she kissed him.

They rolled into each other's arms and began a long passionate kiss. Their hands roamed each other's bodies. In moments they were making love on the sofa. They would fall asleep in each other's arms and it would be early in the morning before they went into the bedroom.

Hong's drive to Kaimuki didn't take long; it was past seven when he left the station and traffic had died down. He stopped at the small deli by his house and picked up dinner, then went home. He hated going home. Too many memories of his wife echoed through the house and it bothered him. Kim had been a beautiful woman and they had been high school sweethearts. They married after college. He had joined the police force and she had gone into law. It made for strange bedfellows at times, especially if he had been the arresting office and she was the defending attorney. They had had no children. Her death had thrown his world out of orbit and for a time, he lost his way. But with Jones' help, he had regained his footing, found the hit-and-run driver, and watched him go to prison.

He sat down at the table and unwrapped his dinner. Quietly he ate in the lonely house as the moonlight began to shine. It was past ten p.m. when he finished and went into the living room. He flopped down on the sofa and flicked on the TV to watch the evening news. He fell asleep before ten minutes had passed.

Morning would find another murder on Hong's desk, just like the first two.

~ ~ ~

Veronica Kekoa had been single, 38 years old, a top-notch realtor making big money, nice figure, nice home and she was dead. It seemed that there was a knife sticking in her nude body. In fact she had been stabbed sixteen times and her throat slit according to the coroner. She had been found in her Waikiki high-rise apartment in the living room. The white shag rug was now brownish-red with blood. Except for that one item the house was spotless, like someone had cleaned it up after killing her.

Jones and Hong read the report and were about to go to the scene of the crime when ace Honolulu Daily News reporter Charlie Kelly came strolling up to their desks.

"Hear we got another dead woman."

"Good news travels fast around here doesn't it, Chuck?" Jones said with a sneer.

Kelly was not well liked around the squad room as he had caused a number of problems with several cases. He did have his uses though and Hong had used him several times before on cases that had given him trouble. A little clue here and there, and a little slip of misinformation had helped track down several criminals.

"Well Charlie, there is nothing we can tell you," Hong said.

"Come on guys. Who has always helped you out? Who has always been there in your times of need? Who has always been the man for you?"

"Do you really want me to answer that Chuck?" came Jones' reply.

"Now CJ he has been a help to us."

Kelly looked happy that Hong was coming to his defense. Charlie and CJ had never gotten along. In fact she had decked him one time because of a comment he made about her chest. Jones was a very well endowed woman.

Kelly, on the other hand was a slime ball.

Jones had spend a week on administrative leave and had to write a letter of apology to Kelly. It was only the beginning and not the end of their on again off again feud. Last week Jones had wanted him arrested for being in a crime screen and possibly disturbing evidence. Hong had talked her out of it.

"I'll tell you what I will do for you Charlie. Whenever we have something new on the case I'll call you first. I promise."

"You are a lot of help."

"Well that's the best I can do for you."

"Just tell me one thing! Is it the same MO?"

"Yes," was all Hong said and walked past him out of the squad room.

"You know, Charlie, one of these days your going to get your foot stuck somewhere it shouldn't be, and I hope I am there, because I'm going to laugh my head off and walk away."

Jones left him standing by the desks.

~~~

Amy rose from bed before John had opened his eyes. She went to the bathroom and turned on the shower, glanced at her nude figure in the mirror and admired herself. She stepped into the shower and felt the warm water pound against her body. A refreshing wave of pleasure over came her and she allowed herself to relax against the shower wall. She soaped her body and then rinsed. She applied shampoo to her hair and rubbed it in smelling the aroma of mango and coconut lather. She rinsed it off, stepped from the shower and toweled off. Wrapping the towel around her she went back into the bedroom and selected her underwear and outerwear for the day. John was still asleep on his side of the bed. She knew he was naked under the satin sheets.

She dressed and went downstairs to make coffee. She had been surprised by John's performance last night. It was far above his general abilities; she smiled to herself as she waited for the coffee to brew. She heard him moving in the bedroom. She poured her coffee and sat down at the breakfast nook and waited.

He arrived dressed in shorts and T-shirt, poured his coffee and planted a kiss on her forehead as he sat down beside her. He took a big drink of the hot coffee and stared out the window at the ocean down below the cliff.

"It's going to be a great day. Look at that sunrise," he said smiling.

"It's nice, honey." She paused then spoke again. "Any plans for the day?"

"No, not really. I am open for anything, How about you? Any thing you want to do?

"Haven't really thought about it," she lied.

"Well how about a drive around the island or a trip to the beach?"

"That would be fine as long as I get to spend some money shopping."

"Why not? We've got it to spend," he said with a laugh. "In fact, let's go out for breakfast and make it a long day. You game?"

She nodded and they left the table. In minutes they were gliding down the hillside headed for one of their favorite restaurants. It was a small local spot away from the tourists—nothing fancy about the place but they liked it. The parking lot was crushed gravel and as they drove in, the tires kicked up a cloud of white dust coating the black BMW with a fine sheet of gravel dust. He helped her out of the car and they walked up to front door of the restaurant. At the door was Kimo, the owner, head chef, and janitor.

"Come for breakfast, Mr. And Mrs. Morris?"

"Yeah, Kimo, what's the special this morning?"

"Same as every day, you know tha'."

The special was eggs, Portuguese sausage, rice, toast, and choice of beverage. It was always the same. Of course you got your eggs anyway you wanted them, as long as it was over easy or sunny side up. It was the "charm" that always brought the Morrises to Kimo's, not necessarily the food. Service at Kimo's was local style: it got there when it got there, and Kimo's daughter, Leialoha, was the only waitress, but she added a very bright spot to the meal, as she was always dressed for the beach in a tiny bikini. John just had to look and Amy punched him lightly on the arm as a reminder that were there together.

When they finished John paid the bill and left a healthy tip on the table. Leialoha gave him a big smile and Amy punched him again, laughing. They hopped in the car and headed down the highway for Honolulu. They passed several local fruit stands and trinket shops for the tourists before Amy spotted a place she frequented and had John pull over and stop. She was out of the car and inside before he had even opened his door. He shook his head, thinking how sometimes she was so much like a little girl. He followed her in. She had already picked out several items and was about to try a beach outfit on.

"You like this one?" she asked, spinning around with it in her hands.

"Well I think I would have to see it on you first."

She smiled and dashed into the changing room with a giggle. It was going to be a great day.

~~~

Forensics was hard at work when the two detectives arrived. It looked the same as the other murder scenes, spotless with a nude body resting in the middle of the dining room floor. Blood was sticky on the hardwood floor. She had been stabbed repeatedly and her throat had been cut. The blood should have splattered all over, but it had been cleaned up, according to the head of the forensic team. Blood was only around the body.

Ms. Kekoa's life had come to an untimely end.

Jones looked around the room. In the far corner sat a computer. She tapped Hong on the shoulder and pointed. They avoided the working forensic team members to get to the computer. Hong touched the computer and saw the same misty views in his head. He leaned into the keyboard and his face strained with pain as it had before, only this time, CJ could see real pain on his face.

He pulled away from the computer and staggered to the dining table behind him, collapsing in a chair.

"CJ, I saw the killing."

"Did you see the killer?"

"No, only a shadow, but I watched the woman having her throat cut. She was sitting at the computer, online I think. She never saw the person. It was gruesome. There should be blood all over the screen and keyboard."

He placed his head in his hands and was silent. Jones stood with her hand on his shoulder, rubbing it softly. He looked up and Jones saw that there were tears in his eyes. She had never seen him so emotional. He responded to her look by turning away. He dabbed his eyes quickly so no one would notice how he had broken down. He then began check the room for any clues that the forensic team might have missed. He was just doing it as a cover; he needed to walk around and pull himself together. He knew Mike Choi and his team were the best in the Honolulu Police Department; they wouldn't miss a thing.

"Well, Jimmy, I think I can safely say she's been dead at least forty-eight hours. Body temperature and rigor don't lie. She was dead before she hit the floor. I can't account for the lack of blood, except to say someone cleaned it up, and they did a damned good job. We found a few splatters on the computer screen and some in the cracks in the wood floor, but other than that, this place is spotless. Not even her fingerprints in this room," Choi said in his matter-of-fact way.

"Was she sexually assaulted?"

"No. Just like the others. You know, Jimmy, I don't get it. Why was she sitting nude at her computer? Or was she murdered and then stripped? You got yourself a real winner out there—a nut case, no doubt about it."

"Yeah, I am afraid so! Can you get the report back to me by tomorrow morning?" Hong asked.

"Sure. Will have the whole thing on your desk in the a.m. Have to run; the room's all yours. We've got everything we're going to find. See you at the station."

Choi left the room followed by his team, leaving Jones and Hong in the middle of the room. The body had been removed and only a white chalk line remained to tell the story of her death—waste. She had been a waste of a person, and for what? Had she ever caused a death or injury? Hong had checked her record, which showed only a traffic violation eight years ago. This lady was just that—a lady.

"Make sure they impound that computer. Let's go."

They rode back in silence. Hong was just sitting, thinking. It was several minutes before he spoke. "CJ, this whole case is wrapped around the computers. Each of them holds the answer to the murders. I am sure of that and I am also sure that there is only one killer. It's the reason that is stumping me. It's right in front of me but I can't see it."

"You will. You always do," she said grimly.

"Well it better be quick. Too many people have died already."

They pulled into the station as Kelly was about to leave. He walked over and leaned into the open window on Hong's side, with a broad grin on his face. You could tell he was full of himself.

"Well, Jimmy, my boy, I got what I needed from Choi. You know he is always very helpful when it comes to a story."

"If you got what you need, why don't you go away," Jones said bitterly.

"Oh, I will, and don't forget to read tomorrow's first edition, lady."

"The son-of-a-bitch. I hate him," was all Jones could say as he walked away.

"Now CJ, there are all kinds of bastards in this world. He can't help himself. Come on. We've got work to do," Hong said, smiling as he stepped out of the car.

On Jones's desk were two large manila envelopes, the names of the first two victims neatly typed on the top right hand corner of each. She opened the first one and began reading:

Both computers have a number of e-mail addresses that are repeated numerous times. I have eliminated most of them because they do not fall in the time frame of the murder. However, three do fall in the time frame.

1) *Richard Yoshiro*
2) *John Morris*
3) *Albert Kong.*

From the data so far, it would appear that one of these three men was talking to her when she was killed.

We are presently continuing to gather information from the computer's hard drive and should have all information available by tomorrow morning.

-Sean Malama-

"Jim, we have three suspects from the computer information Sean has provided. I'll run a check on them now," she said as she handed him the packages and picked up the telephone. "I'll see what the files have on any of the men."

Jim scanned the information and his eyes lit up when he came across Albert Kong. Although a well-known businessman from California, had his roots in the islands. Many of his business operations on the mainland had been on the shady side. Since his arrival in the islands ten years ago, he had kept himself clean of the underworld. True, the California police had been unable to pin anything on him, but everyone knew he was dirty. His money had come from gambling, the protection rackets, and drugs, but murder just didn't fit him.

The other two names on the list were only vaguely familiar. Richard Yoshiro was an insurance tycoon, who created a major financial kingdom in Hawaii by insuring the "uninsurable" for outrageous fees! He made a killing, but again, he was not the type to commit murder outside of the legal business world.

Finally there was Morris, an export/import big wheel with flash, money, and one hell of a beautiful wife, Jim recalled. Their whirlwind romance, wild courtship, and honeymoon had been the talk of the Honolulu social set for months. It was hard to figure Morris as a murderer either.

They had three suspects and yet none of them seemed to be the type to commit the ghastly murders they were investigating. It looked like another dead end. Jones returned with an armful of manila folders and dropped them on her desk.

"Yoshiro and Morris are clean—not even a parking ticket, but Kong has a sheet on him. No convictions, but he has heavy ties to the underworld both here and in California. He was heavy into gambling and drugs while in California, along with some hard-nosed protection rackets. Since returning to Hawaii he has been Mr. Clean. He has a house in Hawaii Kai and a beach house in Lanikai. He's a very private man and stays away from any involvement with the local crime syndicate."

She looked up from the pile of papers and saw Jim with a huge grin on his face. It was easy to see the laughter in his eyes.

"You...already know all this don't you?"

He nodded and she sat down.

"By the way, he came back ten years ago and married a local girl after divorcing his first wife. She returned to California with a very large suitcase filled with bills—the spending kind," Hong said, filling in Jones' report.

"Really, we don't have much. Three men, talking with our victims by computer, doesn't make them murderers. It does, however, put them in line for a visit by the police—us! Grab you sunglasses and let's get going. Let's start with Yoshiro. Got an address?"

"Yes. It's on Kapiolani Boulevard, at The Yoshiro Building, just in Waikiki."

Richard Yoshiro was in his early forties and had been a multimillionaire before he reached twenty-four. He had found that little nitch in life that no one else was filling and he filled it. It wasn't long before he was king of the insurance business in Hawaii. Then he expanded to the mainland and into Japan. He had the right product at the right time and he knew it.

His office was one of those you might see on some Hollywood series with the bad guys doing business right under the cops' eyes and no one noticing. His secretary was right out of *Lovemates*, a second rate men's magazine. She was a bleached platinum blonde with fake green cat's eyes, long fingernails, and a "come hither" look on her face.

"Can I help you?"

"Yes, we need to see Mr. Yoshiro."

"Do you have an appointment?"

"No."

"Well, I'm sorry but Mr. Yoshiro only sees people by appointment. Now I have one available next Wednesday at 3 p.m. Shall I put you and the lady down?"

"I am Detective Lieutenant James Hong and this is Detective Sergeant CJ Jones. This is police business, so why don't you page your boss so we can talk with him."

She sat there staring at the police badge Hong had flipped out. She picked up the phone and spoke softly, nodded, and then her eyes met Hong's.

"Please go right on in."

"See? Sometimes your don't really need an appointment, do you?" Jones said.

If the outer office was impressive, then Yoshiro's was a mansion in a building. No expense had been spared. When they stepped into the room, the first thing that struck them was the desk he was sitting behind. It was ten feet across, made of the finest cherry wood. It dominated the room. The floor-to-ceiling glass windows allowed any visitor to see the beautiful blue waters of the Pacific Ocean and the beach at Waikiki. A large settee was against one wall and the other held a full bar with leaded crystal decanters filled with expensive liquors. Two chairs facing the desk completed the set of furniture in the room. On two walls were paintings, one of Yoshiro and the other a young woman, maybe in her early thirties. Yoshiro rose as they came into the room and greeted them with a smile.

"Lieutenant Hong, Sergeant Jones, what can I do for you?"

"Mr. Yoshiro, we are here on a murder investigation. I am sure you have been reading in the newspaper about the two women found naked in their homes murdered."

"Yes it is terrible, but why come to see me? I didn't know either of the women."

"There you are wrong. In fact, you knew them very well it appears."

"What?"

"Mr. Yoshiro, do you chat online?"

"Well, yes."

"You were chatting with both of the women around the time they were murdered."

"Then I couldn't be the killer. If I was chatting with them, I was miles away. Besides, I don't even know the real names of the people I chat with. Everyone usually uses a fake name or something."

"Do you know a ladyblue@lovesong.net or sweetheart122@lovesong.net'?"

He paused, thinking before he answered. "Yes, I do. Do you mean to tell me those were the two ladies that were killed? Those were the handles of my friends. I swear I didn't know their names! They were just people I chatted with in the evening. They were good friends."

"Yes, and according to the hard drive, you were online with them close to the time they were murdered."

"They were friends. I was just chatting with them."

"Sir, can you verify where you were on the following dates and with whom?" Jones asked, handing him a piece of paper.

He glanced at the paper and then checked his calendar.

"Both days I was here in the office. Ms. Lavender can verify that the first date I was on a flight to Maui around 9 p.m. On the other date, I was home alone—No, wait—I went out that night with some business associates around ten for drinks in Waikiki." He handed the paper back to CJ.

Hong was looking directly into Yoshiro's eyes. "Mr. Yoshiro, I would like you to stay in town until further notice."

"Am I a suspect?"

"Until we can find the killer, anyone that has had a relationship with either of the women is a suspect. Thank you for your time."

Jones and Hong rose and went to the door.

"By the way, do you know either John Morris or Albert Kong?"

"No, can't say I do," Yoshiro answered. "Are they suspects too?"

Hong didn't answer. He opened the door and left. Ms. Lavender was doing her nails as they left The Yoshiro Building. She didn't look up as they left, but Jones watched her wiggle her way into Yoshiro's office, undoing her hair as she went.

It was getting late and they returned to the police station. On Jones' desk was another manila folder. She opened it and read down the data until she stopped at three names, the same three names. Coincidence? She shook her head and handed it to her partner. He only glanced at the sheet of paper and set it on his desk.

"It's in the computers. It's got to be there somewhere. They are being killed for a reason. A crazy reason, but it is a reason in someone's warped mind."

"I agree. I just can't come to any idea of why," CJ said, frowning.

Photos and computer printouts were spread out on their desks, yet both detectives were stumped. After several minutes the room began to empty for the day. Captain Streeter came up behind CJ and stood quietly. It was like he was invisible to the detectives. He broke the silence by reaching for one of the photos.

"You can't bring her back," he said. "No one can bring her back."

They were all staring at the photo of Lita Jackson. Her throat was cut and the look in her eyes was one of horror.

"Go home! That is an order. Go home and come back tomorrow. You both need the sleep and I need two alert detectives, ones that won't miss a clue during their investigations."

Hong reached up and turned off the lamp on his desk as Jones was doing the same. It was already seven p.m. They had been off duty for two hours.

~~~

CJ didn't want to get out of bed the next morning. She had slept like a rock after making love and wanted to go on sleeping and dreaming about the evening, but Rick already had breakfast ready for her on a tray. He sat it down on his side of the bed then gently woke her. A little kiss on the neck and a pat on her butt brought her to life. She rolled over to face him and kissed him back. It was a warm kiss full on the mouth. He knew she was awake.

"Hey, breakfast will get cold."

"Honey, I don't think I really need breakfast. I would rather have something else."

"Well this is what you are going to get." CJ sighed and picked up the fork.

He always treated her extra special when he had the opportunity. He had prepared her favorites: French toast with strawberries, powdered sugar, hot syrup, and bacon, with coffee completing the meal on the tray he set before her. He sat beside her.

She suddenly felt ravished and began eating with great zeal.

"You getting any closer to the murderer?"

"Not yet," she said between bites.

"Maybe you won't want to read *The Daily News* right now then?"

He was holding a copy in his hand. She reached for it and flipped it open to the front page. The banner, which ran across the top of the page read "Police Baffled By Serial Killer" and the secondary headline screamed "Hong, Jones Incompetent."

She crushed the paper and tossed it on the floor. Anger was building in her face and Rick took her in his arms and held her close. The anger suddenly turned to tears and she cried openly. He continued to hold her close. She finally regained control and went to the bathroom to get ready for work. Rick stood by the door as she undressed and slipped into the warm shower.

"Anything I can do?"

"No. Not right now. I have to get ready. You going to be home early tonight?"

"Yes, I should be," came his reply.

"Good! I think it is time we talked about you and me and this job."

"Okay, but relax today. We have all had cases where nothing seems to fit and then, bang! It all falls in place. The kids are up. I'll get them ready."

"Okay," she said.

She stayed in the shower letting the water beat against her and found she was crying again. *That son-of-a-bitch*, she thought. *He prints only half the truth and only the most sensational parts.* She wondered if Jim had read it yet.

Across town, Hong was sitting in the kitchen reading the same story. He was grinning to himself. So Charlie Kelly figured he had a story, did he? Well he was about to have the chair pulled out from under him, with Jimmy Hong doing the pulling. It was enough to take a swing at him, but his partner didn't deserve any of the criticism. He folded the paper in half and placed it on the table, took his dishes to the sink, washed them, and placed them in the rack. He wiped his hands on a towel and scooped up the paper as he walked out the door. He was whistling a tune as backed the car down the driveway. Old Charlie was in for a surprise.

He had just turned out of his driveway when his cell phone rang. He saw it was CJ and answered.

"Good morning, CJ. You read the morning paper yet?"

"Yes, I have. Don't like what he had to say, either."

"Meet me at the office as soon as you can. We need to put him in his place before he destroys our investigation."

"Be there in forty-five minutes. I'm leaving the house now."

She hung up and he glanced at his watch. It was just a minute or so past seven a.m. He would be at the station in ten minutes. A couple of quick calls before seven-thirty and Charlie Kelly would start feeling the pressure from his superiors. Nothing like knowing the right people, in the right places to get things straightened out. Jim pulled into parking lot and went upstairs. The shift had not changed yet. A few people were mingling around. Jim went to his desk. He saw the manila folder marked with Victoria Kekoa on it but elected to make a phone call first. He dialed a number and listened to the metallic ring; then a sleepy voice answered.

"Yeah! Hello? Who is this?" asked an irritated voice.

"Good morning Sam. It's me, Jim Hong." Jim had called the *Honolulu Daily* publisher, Sam Kanehele. He and Sam graduated from the University of Hawaii and their pasts reached even further back, including their high school days at Kaimuki High, and before. They had been friends for a long time. They had played on the football and basketball teams for three years and were always seen together. In fact, they had married sisters. Kim and Elizabeth were almost like twins. Born one year apart, they were like two bookends. Ever since Kim's death, whenever he visited the Kanahele's, he saw Kim in Elizabeth's face. It hurt him to go, but he loved them, so he went numerous times during the year.

"Oh, for crying out loud, Jim! What do you want?"

"Now, Sam, I know its early, but we need to talk."

"Charlie Kelly?"

"You got it. He never seems to get all the facts and goes off half-cocked. He is messing in my investigation. I promised him he would get the real scoop when I had it, and he goes off and prints this fragmented story. Sam, he is hindering us and might even be helping the murderer. Can you do something about it, at least until I can arrest someone? I've got a couple of good leads and I think we might be wrapping things up in a day or so."

Jim had lied, but he needed time and he needed Kelly sitting on the sidelines, not monkeying up the works.

"Okay, Jim, but if you break your word to him, I'll turn him loose."

"You got a deal. Say hello to Liz for me."

"No, you do that; she's right here." Jim heard the rustling of bed sheets and then a voice on the line as soft and sweet as Kim's had been.

"Hi Jim. Where have you been and why haven't you been by to see us? You are being a naughty boy." *Just like Kim,* he thought, *always being the loving, caring person to everyone.*

"Sorry, Liz, but I've been very busy of late. I promise to make it over there soon, okay?"

"Well you better. I have a big kiss waiting for you and a bigger hug. We will see you soon. Love you very much."

"Love you too." There was a dial tone and Jim hung up.

Jones came in and sat down. She had a pained look on her face.

"CJ, I have taken care of our friend for now."

"Thanks. I was about to drive by the *Daily* and punch him in the nose."

"Good thing you didn't; I would hate to have to bail you out of jail."

"Actually, I think the guys would have pinned a medal on me just for thinking about hitting him."

Jim nodded. He picked up the manila folder he had forgotten about and opened it. It was the computer printout information from the last victim's computer. He quickly scanned the report until he stopped. The same three names were on the list as having contacted her. He handed it to CJ, pointing at the names.

"Our duo is now a trio, and all three of our suspects have had contact with the dead women."

CJ took the other folders out of her desk and spread the contents of each folder out. Photos, forensic reports, and computer printouts all pointed at one of the three suspects as the murderer, but who? Which one of them was guilty? This evidence alone was not going to convict anyone. They both knew it. They needed more from the computer geek downstairs. Malama would have to dig deeper in each of the computers to come up with the answers they needed.

"I'll go down and talk with Malama. We going to visit our other two suspects today as well?"

"Yeah. Hurry and get back. I want to see Morris this morning and Kong this afternoon. One of them might shed a little light on the murders."

Jones left the room and Jim went back to looking at the evidence on the desks. Three lives had come to a sudden end and he and CJ had to find the killer before he struck again. The killings were brutal and yet in the aftermath, someone went to a get deal of trouble to clean it up. It was like two different people involved with the murder. One, a brutal, satanic demon, and the other, a cleaning woman, who could not stand to leave a place messy. It was bewildering to say the least. A cleanup on that scale would have taken hours. Whoever killed the women was a cool cucumber. He didn't worry about anyone interrupting him, nor did he seem to mind if anyone saw him. Witnesses didn't report any strangers in the areas or even near the scenes. It was like someone came in like a wisp of smoke and left the same way. He recalled many Chinese and Japanese tales of ghosts and demons, but he couldn't recall any as horrible as these. He wondered if the killer was watching his victims close up. If so how was he selecting which ones to kill? There had to be one link that would tie them all together.

Jones had returned but Hong was frozen on the evidence. He was trying to find anything to give him an idea where to go.

"Jim, you ready to leave?"

"Yeah let's get going, long day ahead," he said.

Ms. Puanani was at her computer, working on some shipping orders. Hong and Jones entered and waited for her to turn around. As she did, her eyes fell on their badges.

"We'd like to see Mr. Morris. We're Detectives Hong and Jones."

"One minute, sir." She called him on the phone. "Mr. Morris, Detectives Hong and Jones are here to see you."

She nodded hung up the phone and the directed them to his door.

John Morris sat behind his desk and waited for the two detectives. He didn't say a word. In fact he didn't look up at them.

"What can I do for you?" he said with his face buried in some papers on his desk.

"Answer a few questions to start," Hong replied.

Morris finally looked up to face the detectives for the first time. He viewed the two as a nuisance, something interrupting him from his business. He usually swatted any nuisance away as he would do to a fly that was bothering him. Today, however, he had read the morning issue of *The Honolulu Daily*, which was still sitting on his desk, and he knew who the two officers were. How could any one miss a blazing headline like that? He was still irritated by the intrusion.

"I am Detective Hong and this is Detective Jones. Do you have a computer in your home?"

"Detective Hong, I couldn't survive without a computer in my home. It's a lifeline to my business. Are you investigating me in relation to the murders I have been reading about?"

"Yes. In fact, with what we have, you and two other men are prime suspects in the case."

"Are you out of your mind? I don't even know those three women! This is an outrage. How dare you insinuate that I have anything to do with these murders?"

"Unfortunately, that isn't true. You see, you have been talking to all three women via your computer and not just once, but many times." He handed Morris a list of the e-mail addresses and watched the man's face change. He could tell that Morris had been struck by lightning.

"I didn't know. We had just been chatting online, but just because I am someone that talked with them doesn't mean I killed them. Come on, detectives, isn't this a little lame? I mean how could I kill them and be talking on the net with them at the same time?"

"You have a point, Mr. Morris, but you see, they were killed, as best we can figure, after chatting with you or one of the other two men on our list."

"Detective Hong, I will be happy to cooperate with the police in any way possible. I have nothing to hide. Because I didn't do it."

Hong was pretty sure at this point that Morris really didn't do it. He had reacted like anyone innocent. He didn't appear to be playing a game or avoiding the issues, but still he was a prime suspect. Before leaving, Hong told Morris to stay in town. As Hong and Jones turned to leave, Morris returned to his paper work not even saying good-bye to the detectives.

After they left, Morris turned to his computer and typed in one of the addresses on the list. It showed that it was not in use. The owner was not available and that was the truth. She really wasn't available she was dead.

The drive to Albert Kong's beach house was about an hour. In route they went over every detail of the case, nit-picking every item about each of the crime scenes. They were looking for a reason for the murders. Usually a reason was obvious, but there seemed to be no reason. No money was taken, none of the women had been raped or assaulted sexually, and none of them seemed to have any enemies. In fact, they were loners, even in their own offices. And why were they naked when they were found? All these questions just seemed to pile more questions on questions.

The drive across the Pali Highway was scenic to say the least. The rain forest that the highway passed through was alive with color, both floral and fauna. If you watched closely you saw every variety of flower in Hawaii along the roadside and clinging to the trees. The brightly colored bird that flew from tree to tree filled the air with flight and song. It was easy to become lost in this world of magnificence. They passed through the Pali tunnel and broke out on the other side to the low rolling hills of Kailua. They passed the turn off to Kaneohe and headed for Kailua town.

Kailua still held a little of *old* Hawaii in it, although it too was growing up far too fast for many of the locals as well as the kamainas. Jim remembered the time when there was only one stoplight in the entire town and a traffic jam might have been half a dozen cars trying to make the turn from Kailua Road onto Pali Highway. He smiled and grinned.

"Let's get something to eat. I know a little place that makes great plate lunches."

CJ nodded and followed Hong's directions to a small deli off the beaten path, but well-attended by those that knew about it. The screen door was closed yet the aroma of food drifting out the door could be smelled from the door, drawing in customers for lunch. Behind the counter, two little Japanese ladies were making luncheon plates for laborers, while others waited in line for their turn.

Each plate was piled with local favorites, like teriyaki chicken, steak or pork, fish, Spam, rice, potato salad, and pickled Japanese vegetables, plus other items not found in some restaurants in the islands. You could tell how well-liked the food was by the number of people waiting to be served. It was small inside, with just a few tables and chairs, but generally people picked up their lunches and sat outside in the fresh air and sunshine.

The detectives ordered their plates and went outside to eat, sitting at a picnic table, enjoying the beautiful Hawaiian day. The clouds drifted in the sky like white puffs of smoke against a deep blue sea. The breeze blew softly against their faces and the sun felt warm. They ate in silence, enjoying the peaceful world around them—in high contrast to the world they usually lived in.

The short ride from the deli to the Kong's beach house through Kailua and then Lanikai was like going back into the past. The bridge leading to Lanikai was as it always was—filled with people coming and going to the beaches. Canoes slid through the water and swimmers leaped from the bridge and sunbathers lay on the sand under the tropic sun.

The large white gates were closed when they arrived. The guard at the guardhouse asked their business and called the house. The massive gate swung open to a well-manicured lawn, house near the beach, and several cars parked in the front drive. Two men with aloha shirts on met them at the door. They both were carrying concealed weapons, which bulged out. Hong also noticed a man on the roof with an automatic weapon. They had driven into a fortress, not a beach house.

"Good afternoon. Mr. Kong is at the pool. Please follow this man. He will take you to him." The servant was a young Hawaiian man in his early twenties. He didn't say a thing, only opened doors and gestured where to go. They passed through the house. It was filled with oriental antiques mixed with avant-garde furniture. Crystal glass was everywhere and flowers covered the tables.

Sitting in a lounge chair next to a bikini-clad woman was Albert Kong, in his mid-fifties, with coal black hair and features of a man who had fought in a number of wars. He was wearing reflective sunglasses and had a drink in his hand.

"Care for a drink? Mai tai or something harder?"

"No thanks; we're on duty."

"How can I help you? I figure you are here regarding the three murders. Well, number one, I can account for my whereabouts for the last sixty days. I have a number of people known and unknown to you that will vouch for me. Secondly, I didn't know any of the women to begin with."

"Mr. Kong, could we speak in private?"

"I don't have any secrets to hide from anyone."

"Well then let me break the bad news to you. You knew all three women! You knew them on the internet. You talked with them on a regular basis and you were talking to them at and around the times they were killed." The girl in the bikini leaped from the chair and flew into the house, steam issuing from her ears and calling Kong every vile name you could think of. He eased back into his lounger and glared

"Listen, you'd better have some strong evidence to prove what you are saying, or my lawyers will make retirement something you will beg for."

"We have the proof. It was in their computers and it should be in yours."

He played with his drink, looking straight out to sea. Hong watched him closely for any movement that might revel what he was thinking. Finally Kong turned and took off his sunglasses. His dark black eyes peered at Hong. "I was there and I didn't have anything to do with it. So get the hell out of here now." He signaled to several men and they approached with hands held near where their weapons were.

"Thanks for your time, and don't leave town," Jones said as they were escorted back to the house. As they walked through the house, the bikini-clad woman bumped into Jones. During the encounter she slipped a note into the detective's hand and gave her an angry look. Jones closed her hand on the note and followed the escorts to the waiting car.

Hong was in the driver's seat, not the usual way for them to travel, and Jones slid in beside him. Hong started the car and headed for the closed gates. He waited until they opened it and then drove through, watching in the rearview mirror as it closed. Then he turned to CJ. "What did she give you?"

"A note," she said. She opened her hand to see a crumpled piece of pink paper. On the paper was a phone number—*808-555-2376*—and the words *call after 10 p.m., Dixie*.

"Well, someone wants to talk about something privately," Jones said.

~ ~ ~

Amy Morris was sitting on the bed. She was waiting for a call from John. They had made plans for evening. She was dressed in black panties and bra, doing her toenails. Music was blaring from the entertainment center. She wasn't listening. Besides doing her nails, she was reading a printout from her agent. He had set up another photo shoot for her on the Big Island next month. They would be doing a volcano background layout for a new line of swimsuits. She bounded off the bed and stood looking at herself in the full-length mirror on the door. She still had a great body and her cascading hair accented her luscious curves. *Why would any man look at another woman, if they had me?* she thought. She jumped back on the bed and lay back on the satin pillow. She felt warm all over. She had the best man in the islands and she knew how to keep him. She let her hands roam over her body and giggled to herself. Yes, she knew how to take care of her man. The doorbell rang and broke the mood. She put on a gown and went to answer it. It was John's secretary.

"Ms. Puanani, what are you doing here?"

"I'm sorry, but Mr. Morris won't be able to get here for dinner. He asked me to bring these flowers to you. He was in a meeting and couldn't get free." She handed Amy a bouquet of white roses, turned, and walked away. She had a sexy walk and that irritated Amy.

The bitch, she thought as Puanani started her car and drove away. Amy wasn't sure, but she thought John was screwing the little bitch, or she was screwing him to keep her job. Either way, Amy would't let it go on. If she could find out what the bitch was doing, she was going to rip every hair out of her head, one strand at a time. She closed the door slowly, looked at the flowers, dropped them on the floor, and walked away.

~ ~ ~

John Morris was sitting behind his computer sending a personal message to a lady in Kaneohe. He had just met her on the internet. She called herself Hotladybelle 4 love. They had been talking for about a week and he enjoyed the time with her. She seemed nice and loved to talk with him. She also was into cyber sex with him, often sitting at her computer and teasing him about what she wasn't wearing. She liked to be called Belle online.

They had been sending messages back and forth for over an hour and the conversation had been hot and heavy from the start. She had begun it by saying she was naked and John had responded, telling her how beautiful she looked, even though he couldn't see her. They laughed and "made love" in cyber space.

They were about to sign off, when Morris got a "be right back" message. He waited until he saw Belle was typing a message. What appeared on his screen ripped his mind away from him. In large letters it read, *"I JUST KILLED YOUR LOVER."* Could it mean that another woman was dead on the internet? If it did, John Morris was right in the middle of murder—murder by e-mail. He sat staring at the screen the words flashing at him. He was hypnotized. He was involved, but *how* was he involved? Finally, he reached for the telephone and called the police. He talked to Lieutenant Hong.

It was only a half hour before Hong and Jones were in his office, along with the forensic crew. The forensic team had his computer apart and out of the room in minutes. Morris was still in a state of shock and couldn't think straight. He didn't respond well to questioning; his mind wandered. He walked around the room muttering under his breath. Then, confused, he turned to the window and stood gazing out on Waikiki, before beginning to pace back and forth. His eyes never met the detectives'.

He was in mid-stride when he blurted out, "I didn't kill her. How could I? I was chatting with her when it happened. The message appeared on my screen. I called the police. Oh my God, that woman is dead, I just know it."

"Well if she is, you have an ironclad alibi," Jones said.

He went back to his pacing, again not looking at anyone, lost in his own world—a world shattered by a simple five-word message on his computer.

Lieutenant Hong's cell phone rang and he answered.

"Hong…Yes…Okay. When can you have all the information from his computer?…All right, we will be returning to the station with Mr. Morris. Try to have it on my desk ASAP." He closed the phone.

"Mr. Morris, it appears that your computer will provide the evidence that you couldn't have killed any of the women. We would like you to come down to the office and tell us as much as you can about the times you talked with the women, including the one today. By the way, her real name was Luann Yung. She was 35 and lived in Kailua. She was very wealthy, never worked a day in her life. Inherited the money from her father."

"So that was her name. I just knew her as 'sexyme@lovesong.net'," he said, turning back to the window.

"I better call Amy and tell her I will be a little late tonight."

"You can make the call from the station," Jones said.

Morris looked at her as she took his arm and they left the office.

It was all routine at the office, with Morris providing all the information he could. It was well past 10 o'clock when he left, after being told not to talk to anyone about the investigation. He left without making a call to his wife. Perhaps he didn't want her involved this early, besides, when she did find out about him and his online loves, all hell was going to break loose. He had a hanged-dog look on his face as he left.

Now the spotlight appeared to have shifted to the other two suspects. It wouldn't take long now before they had their killer in custody, Hong thought.

"CJ, you make that call to Dixie?"

"No, I forgot. I'll do it now."

She punched in the numbers and the phone rang. A small voice answered.

"Hello, is this Dixie Kong?"

"Yes," came the reply. CJ put the phone on conference call. Hong leaned forward to listen.

"This is Detective Jones. You slipped me a note this afternoon and asked me to call."

"Yes. I remember. I know I was upset about my husband's activities but I know he didn't do it. Several years ago after he returned to the islands, one of the California kingpins had a contract out on him. He was shot four times in the back before the bodyguards killed the assassin. The assassin was weighted down, dumped in Kaneohe bay and became fish food. My husband was secretly transported off the island to Japan for major surgery. To sum it all up, he can't walk and hasn't been able to for three years. If you supenoa the medical records from the Tokyo Medical Center in Japan, it can be proven. I love him so very much, but I was so mad right then; I had to leave. He feels he isn't a man now and I knew he wouldn't say anything to you about it. Besides, there is the assassin in Kaneohe Bay. And if you ever say I gave you this information, I will call you liars to your faces."

"Thank you, Mrs. Kong. I don't think it would be to our advantage to dredge up a skeleton. Besides, as you say, we didn't hear it from you. Good evening," Hong said and Jones hung up the phone.

"That just leaves Yoshiro," Jones said.

"Yes. I guess it does."

"Shall we go make an arrest?"

"CJ, there is something wrong here. Let's wait until tomorrow. I have a hunch about this. Not all the pieces are in the puzzle, because if they are, somebody has been playing with them."

They turned off their lights and headed home.

~ ~ ~

The *Honolulu Daily* had an interesting lead story the next morning. Richard Yoshiro was dead. His private plane had crashed leaving Maui Airport for Honolulu around 8 p.m. There were no survivors. He had been attending a meeting of mainland investors for his latest money-making venture. He had arrived on Maui the night before. This left Hong and Jones high and dry, out of the water, back to square one.

The article also brought Charlie Kelly out of his rat hole, looking for a story. He figured someone owed him something and he was going to collect. His boss had put a muzzle on him and he knew either Hong or Jones had put him up to it. He figured it was Hong, since Kanehele and Hong were related by marriage. He was pissed off about it and wanted to get back at them. He had never been muzzled before and he didn't like it.

Kelly knew that Hong and Jones had three suspects and he knew their names. Kelly also knew that Morris and Kong were still in the mix, but that Yoshiro was a dead duck, literally. His sources had been providing him with detailed information on the investigation. From the data, he came up with his selection for the murderer.

With Yoshiro eliminated, Kelly was weighting his information to find out who the killer was, in his little mind.

He figured Kong was the best prospect for murdering the women, yet he had heard rumors that Kong wasn't the man he used to be and maybe didn't have the power to knock someone off anymore.

Morris was his third choice. Kelly had his sources on Morris, as he did on everyone in the islands. Morris was a workaholic, but was always seen with his wife at every island function, and she was a beauty. A former model with a head on her shoulders for business, she had helped her husband triple his business.

What was hanging Kelly up was a motive. No one had one!

~ ~ ~

The same thing was making Hong and Jones scratch their heads. It had looked like they had finally pinned Yoshiro down as the killer, but then he had gotten himself killed in a plane crash. Kong was paralyzed and couldn't move without help, and Morris was at his desk when the murder was committed. Three strikes, they were out.

CJ was tapping the eraser end of her pencil on the desk, reading the reports on the four murdered women, looking for a link. Suddenly the lights went on in her head. She looked up at Jim, smiling.

"Maybe we are looking for the wrong sex here."

"What do mean?"

"We have been saying 'he' all the time. Maybe it is a 'she' we should be looking for."

Hong's eyes cast a deep penetrating look at her. "You may be right, CJ, but it's hard to image a woman being as brutal as this murderer has been. You read the report on the last one stabbed twenty times and throat slit?"

"Yes, I have read it. But look at the neatness. It could be someone with a fetish for cleanliness, but I don't think so. I think it's a woman—someone that does the murder out of rage, then has to clean up the mess to make it go away in her mind."

"But why not a man?"

"Men like things neat and clean, but don't go that extra step. Remember the smell at the first three murder scenes? It was a household cleaner. I checked in the kitchen at two of the three scenes we were at; the odor was the same. It was mixture of several cleaning fluids. I know I use it in my own home: Pinaway, bleach, and lemon juice."

Hong leaned back in his chair, eyes closed, thinking.

"Jim, our killer is a woman!"

"If it is a woman, which one? It could be any one of maybe fifty or sixty contacts. It doesn't have to be the wife of any of our three suspects, who aren't suspects anymore."

"You saw how Kong's wife reacted when you told him about his online activities!"

"Yeah, but she's the one that clued us in on his inability to walk. If she were doing the killings, her actions that day would point to her. CJ, she's a smart cookie. If she is the one doing the killing, then we are going to have a hard time proving it."

CJ nodded her head.

"CJ, the only way are going to be able to prove who is killing these women is to catch them in the act. To do that, we are going to have to have—" he stopped in mid sentence. CJ was looking at him with a little smile creeping across her face.

"I don't think so, CJ."

"Why not?"

"I just don't think so. We could use a man disguised as a woman."

"Hell, Jim. If the killer is stalking the victim, no man can pull it off; at least no officer in the force. Only a woman could."

Hong sat back in his chair playing with his pencil. This was a fight he knew he wasn't going to win. When CJ had made up her mind to do something, it was useless to try to talk her out of it. Hong continued to play with his pencil, staring across the desk at his partner. There was dead silence as they looked at each other. He finally gave a sigh and put the pencil down.

"Okay. I'll talk to the chief and see what we can do. I won't guarantee that he will agree, but I will talk to him about you going undercover."

"He'll agree! I know he will."

That ended the discussion and the day for the two detectives. They went their separate ways that evening.

Jones headed home to talk with Rick. She had thought about telling him she was going to hang it up, but now her mind raced with the thoughts of capturing a killer. She felt a rising passion in her body. It was the excitement of placing herself in harm's way. She wanted to be in Rick's arms making love to him.

She pulled into the driveway and got out of the car. She saw the light from the kitchen door beam out and Rick standing with light behind him, making an eerie glow on the driveway. She bounded up the stairs and into his arms. She was filled with desire. She kissed him, closing the door with her foot as she pushed him back into the kitchen. He was in his pajamas and she took full advantage of him there on the kitchen table. Her passion flowed like an uncontrollable torrent of water rushing down a narrow ditch. She thrust her body against his, moving him up onto the table. She released him from his pajamas and shed her pants and panties on the floor. She was on him like a tigress and he responded. They made mad, passionate love on the table, moaning and gasping for breath. They were taken back to their younger days, before the children, when every night was filled with desire and love-making. He lifted and rolled her on her back and now was expressing his own desires. They kissed. They made love until she let out a low moan and collapsed, pulling him down on her. Their bodies were covered with perspiration and they were breathing hard, bodies entwined and united.

"It was good," she said running her fingers through his sweat-coated hair. She kissed him on the forehead.

He lifted his head and gazed into her sea-blue eyes. "Yes it was. Like in the past." He leaned back, gained his balance, then scooped her up and carried her into the bedroom. She wrapped her arms around his neck and gave him little kisses of desire. They wouldn't be talking about anything tonight except love.

~ ~ ~

Hong stopped at a local bar in Kaimuki. It was small and the clientele strictly local couples. He knew the place well. He and Kim frequented it often when they dating and after their marriage. He took a seat at the bar and asked for a beer. The bartender, Matty, poured the brew in a frosted glass.

"Hey, you having bad time, brah?"

"It's always a bad time when I can't solve the crime," Hong responded.

"Hey, no worries. You get the buggar."

Matty was always positive about Hong's abilities when it came to being a detective.

"You no come around no more. Where you stay?"

"Most of the time at the station. This case we have right now is driving me up the walls."

"Yeah I know. Da tree dead wahines, no make tings good. Even the locals no like come out drink. Afraid they might get kill when they get home."

Matty was a throw-back to the days of old Hawaii. He still spoke pidgin English. The bar had been passed down to him from his father and his father before him. They had left the plantation life behind, but not the language.

Hong's grandparents had come from China and had spent their entire working life on the plantations as well. Hong's father had made sure his boy would not grow up, as he had to do. It was good schools from kindergarten to college and nothing was spared to make sure he made it. Often the only meal on the table was rice and beans, but Jim had the books he needed and tutors if it required it.

Hong liked the bar and Matty. It reminded him of his roots. He could go there and be home again, even if only for a short time. Matty moved down the bar to serve another customer, leaving Hong by himself. He sat a long time, nursing the beer and watching the television that droned endlessly on, adding more noise to the chaotic din. He didn't notice the Asian lady when she sat down beside him and ordered a cocktail. He did notice her perfume. It was too heavy and cut the air like a knife.

She tried to start a conversion but Hong's mind was far away. After a minute or so she moved on down the bar and hooked up with another man. They drank several drinks and then left together, his arm wrapped around her waist and his hand on her butt. She gave Hong an eyeful as she passed, and then smiled.

"Want another, brah?" Matty was back from his tour of the bar.

"No. I think I'll call it a night."

"Mahalo, come again. No be stranger, you know!"

Hong walked back to his car and drove home to his empty house. He didn't bother with dinner, just plopped down on the sofa and flipped on the TV to catch the news. He was asleep in minutes.

~~~

John Morris stayed in bed. He was weak from lack of sleep. Lying on his side, his eyes open and vacant, he didn't respond to Amy's voice calling him softly to join her. She was in one of her moods, wanting, desiring, and demanding him to service her. She jabbed him in the back but he didn't move.

"Leave me alone. I don't feel good," was all he said.

Amy turned on her side facing the other way. She didn't, however, remain there long.

"You son-of-a-bitch. You only care about yourself. You don't care about me. I have my needs you know."

He had heard this story too many times before. He shut her ravings out of his mind and drifted back to his office and the computer. A woman he knew was dead, slashed and stabbed to death while he was talking with her. He couldn't get it out of his mind. He briefly heard her rantings again. They were reaching the stage when she would be saying how bad a lover he was. He closed his eyes and ignored her. The final stage was just moments away, if she followed the usual routine. He felt her hands on his back, lightly stroking and her fingers making little patterns on his back. Now gentle kisses began to replace the finger patterns. She pressed her naked body against him and rubbed gently, at the same time pulling him on his back. He didn't care. It didn't matter what she was doing; he could only see the words flashing on his computer screen.

She rolled him on his back and he could see her luscious, firm breasts inches from his face. Her eyes peered down at him, inviting him to kiss them. He just lay there. She broke into a wild tantrum, spilling out hatred as he had never heard before. Sitting on his stomach, she slapped his face repeatedly, then sprang from the bed and stomped out of the room.

John remained in bed the rest of the day, while below, Amy threw dishes and cussed a blue streak.

~~~

CJ woke before Rick did. She propped herself up on one elbow and watched him sleep. *He has a cute little-boyish charm when he's asleep,* she thought. Smiling, she used her fingernail to gently touch his nose and trace a line down to his lips. He waved his hand as if trying to chase away a fly. She waited then repeated her playful touching. This time he caught CJ's hand before she could withdraw from his reach. He pulled her to him and kissed her. They laughed as they broke the embrace and cuddled close, naked under the sheets.

"Hon, I have something to tell you," she said meekly.

"What? I wasn't any good last night?"

She playfully pushed him away and the sheet drifted to the floor. Rick' eyes gazed at her rich, full body with desire, but CJ pulled up the sheet from the floor and stopped him cold.

"No! We have to talk." She paused. "I think I will be starting a new assignment in the next few days and, well, it will be dangerous—very dangerous."

Rick looked at her, his mind twisting and turning with thoughts of apprehension. "Does it have to do with the murders?" he asked.

She could only nod her head.

There was silence in the room. He rolled out of bed, his back turned to her. She crawled across and placed her warm body against his back and wrapped her arms around him, tugging him toward her. She kissed him softly on the shoulder and caressed him until he turned and they slipped back into the still-warm sheets. If their love-making the night before had been rapture, then the next hour was pure ecstasy. CJ would be late to work.

~ ~ ~

Hong awoke still dressed in his work clothes. He had had a rough night and wasn't looking forward to the day ahead.

Captain Streeter would be his first opponent of the day. He knew the old man would scream until the walls shook. Streeter would say no, no, no, but in the end would give in and agree to put CJ on undercover duty—very hazardous undercover duty.

He showered, shaved, and got dressed. He ate a quick breakfast and headed to the station. He met Captain Street going into the building.

"Captain, I need to talk with you."

Streeter paused at the door. Anytime Hong had something serious to talk about, he used Streeter's title, not his name. Like many of the older officers, Hong and Streeter were close friends as well as police officers.

"When you start off that way, Jim, it must be serious. Let's go to my office." Hong closed the office door and sat down.

"I want to put CJ undercover," he blurted out.

A shocked look came across Streeter's face. "What?"

"CJ has come up with the idea that the murderer is a not a man but a woman, and I agree. But to find the murderer, we are going to put some bait out there. CJ wants to do it."

Streeter did not react as Hong had thought he would. Folding his hands on the desk, he looked hard across at Hong. "Can we protect her 24/7?"

"I think we can."

"All right, then get the ball rolling and let's find our murderer and stop her."

Meeting complete, Hong went to his desk. CJ hadn't arrived yet. He called the undercover unit and talked with Ann Simmons. They set up coverage for CJ on the job. He then had the various departments find and rent an apartment, so CJ could set up housekeeping. By the time CJ arrived, everything a young female on the rise would want, was in place, including an upscale apartment in a ritzy locale. She had a job and a new name. Of course she would have to dye her hair to change her appearance somewhat. Clothes came from the property room, as well as money. It was almost ten o'clock when she slid into her chair.

Hong glanced at his watch but said nothing.

"Okay, I'm late. What did the boss say?"

Hong looked up from his paper work and smiled.

"When do I start?"

"Two days. I figure it will take you that long to move in, dye your hair, and start your new job, Ms Cindy Wineberger."

"Shit. You couldn't come up with a better name than that?"

"We all have to suffer a little," he replied.

For eleven years, CJ had wanted to work undercover and now she had her chance. It was risky, but it was something she wanted to do.

"You will be covered every minute you are on this case. Ann Simmons has begun to set up the detail now. Clothes, money, and anything else you will need will come out of property room. You need to change your appearance. Dye your hair, buy a wig, become a redhead, wear glasses—anything so CJ Jones disappears and Cindy Wineberger comes to life. You will still carry your piece at all times. I suggest carrying it somewhere you can get to quickly, in other words, not in your purse.

CJ was drinking it all in. She wondered why Jim was being so formal about the plan. Generally he was easy going and laid back, but now he was talking at her like she was a rookie. It took her a second or two before it popped into her head. Jim was scared. He was afraid of what could and might happen on this undercover assignment. He was acting like the concerned father or husband. She smiled to herself and continued to listen as he rambled on about every little detail. *What a darling to think about me that way*, she thought. He really was afraid for her. She came out of her daydream when he asked, "Any questions?"

She shook her head.

"Good. Now get ready. Take the day off and change into Cindy Wineberger!"

He went back to his paperwork and CJ left.

Hong talked with Malama and they set up CJ's contact name at *lovesong.net*. She would be *aprilblossom@lovesong.net*. and would have to make a connection with John Morris.

The next part of the plan called for Morris to become involved, or at least at his computer. Hong phoned Morris's office but he was not in. The secretary, Ms. Puanani, said he hadn't been in for two days and she had called his home but there had been no answer. She was worried because it wasn't like him to not be at his office two days in a row. She commented that he often came in during the weekends to do work. Hong asked for the home phone and then hung up.

He was wondering if Morris had left town or if something else had happened. He hated to have to drive out to his place, but he had no other choice. He had a uniform officer follow him. The trip took over an hour.

The house impressed Hong. It was two-stories, built to overlook the bay and the sunrise in the morning. It had a look of the old Hawaiian plantation homes of the landowners. It brought back memories of his younger days. He rang the doorbell and waited. Finally the voice came from inside, asking who it was.

"Lieutenant James Hong, Honolulu Police, would like to speak with Mr. John Morris."

The door slowly opened and there stood Mrs. Amy Morris. She smiled and invited Hong and the officer in. As impressive as the outside was, the inside overwhelmed anyone who had never been in the house before. The furniture and decor reeked of money.

"How can I help you?" she asked.

"As I said, I need to speak with Mr. Morris. Is he home?"

"Yes, but I am afraid he is still asleep. He worked late last night at the office."

Hong knew she was lying. Morris's secretary had said he hadn't been in for two days. Why would she lie to him, he wondered.

"Well, Mrs. Morris, it's very important. Would you please wake him?"

Before she could say a word, John Morris appeared at the top of the stairs with a robe on.

"I'm awake. What can I do for you?"

"We need to speak in private, Mr. Morris."

"Fine. Come in the study with me." He pointed the way and the two went in. Morris closed the door behind them and sat down behind his desk.

"We are going to need your help," Hong began. "We are going to need you to carry on a relationship with another online lady."

Morris went white as a sheet. Fear welled up in his face and he began to shake his head.

"I can't do that. I can't put another person in jeopardy. My God, man, don't you realize that four women have already been killed because of me? How can you ask me to do something like that?"

"Mr. Morris, I know this puts a tremendous strain on you, but be reassured the woman who you will be talking with is a trained police officer and has volunteered to help catch the killer by going undercover."

Morris was still reluctant to become involved. It took more time and assurances that the officer would be protected all the time before he finally agreed to work with Hong and his team.

"Mr. Morris, how long had you been talking to the ladies before—well, before they were found dead?"

"I don't recall exactly but I would say at least two or three weeks."

"Well that gives us a time frame to work in then. Where did you talk to the women from—here or at the office?"

"Generally at the office, late in the evening, but I did chat with each of them off and on here, when I was alone."

Hong shook his head. "Well tomorrow, you need to contact this person by e-mail and begin a chat. I want you to talk with her as you did all the others. Same topics, same questions, everything you talked about with the others."

"We got into some heavy sexual items during our talks," Morris said, looking down at the desk.

"If you did, then include them as well. The officer will be advised on how to handle any situation that may come along."

We usually had our cams in play as well. You know, so we could see each other," he paused. "Naked."

So, thought Hong, *this is why the women were naked when murdered.* He had a kinky way about him. CJ is really not going to like this one. "I don't think we have to go that far, but you can request it, as I am sure you did with the others," Hong said.

Morris had his head in his hands and wasn't moving.

"Tell your wife if she asks that we came out because of a series of break-ins near your building and we were concerned that something might have happened in your office, but had not been reported as of yet."

"Sure, I'll do that."

"Be at work tomorrow and let's get this charade started. The sooner we start, the quicker we can find and arrest the killer. I want to thank you for your help in this matter." Hong rose to leave when Morris spoke up.

"Is the officer undercover your partner?"

Hong stopped. "Yes," was all he said, and then left.

After the officers had departed Amy came into the study. She slid her hand on his shoulder and rubbed it gently.

"Everything all right, honey?" she spoke as if nothing had happened the day before. She could feel his muscles tighten under her fingertips. He could never lie to her if she had her hands on his body. He was too emotional and he physically revealed himself to her that way.

"Something about break-ins around the area. They wanted to check if we had had anything happen in our building," he said.

She felt his muscles twitch. He was lying, but why? She kissed him on the head and hugged him, then left the room. She had things to do and places to go before noon.

~~~

CJ had gone down to property room and selected a wardrobe from items taken in raids by the police. Included in her "shopping trip" were several diamond rings, diamond earrings, and a diamond watch. The finest dresses came off the racks, along with shoes to match. It looked like she had won the lottery. The officer in charge kept telling her she was responsible to return everything she was taking. She only nodded and kept on taking things as he made a list, which grew and grew.

It took three trips to her car to finally get everything she had selected from the property room stashed away. She laughed to herself thinking about how Rick was going to flip out when he saw the backseat and truck filled with the clothes and jewelry. He would probably think she had gone over the deep end and had gone into a life of crime.

She giggled again as she pulled into the driveway. No one was home. She emptied the car and scattered the clothing on the bed in their bedroom. Stripping out of her work clothes, she put on a black slip and began trying on dresses and jewelry, looking at herself in the full-length mirror. She turned this way and that, lifting the hem to check its appearance in the mirror. The silk dresses felt good against her skin. She liked the feeling. Although some of the clothes were a little tight in the bust, they were otherwise perfect.

On her police salary and Rick's commissions, she didn't have anything in her own closet to match some of the clothes lying on the bed. She suddenly felt bad about what she was thinking. They always got along with what they had. She didn't need any of these things, besides they were just props for the job she was doing.

She unzipped the dress she was wearing and let it slip to the floor. She picked it up and laid it on the bed. Sure it was nice, but it really wasn't her. She was a cop—a *good* cop and she knew it. If she ever needed a silk dress she would buy it herself or Rick would surprise her with one. She had to remember it was a job, an assignment, the one she had asked for. The door opened and Rick came in. He stopped and looked at the mass of clothes spread out in the room.

"You rob a bank?" he said with a laugh.

"No. These are the clothes for the assignment," she said.

Rick stopped laughing and took her into his arms.

They stood in the middle of the bedroom swaying back and forth as if music was playing softly in the room. She moved against him and they pressed their bodies together, moving to the unknown song filling their minds. She laid her head against his shoulder and her hands clutched his neck, then they looked into each other's eyes and fell more in love than they had been the day before. They danced under a spell that filled them with happiness. The spell was only broken by the sound of the children coming home from school. They raced into the bedroom, knowing their mother was home. They yelled at the tops of their voices, wanting to tell her about their day.

Harley, the littlest, held her arms out so CJ could pick her up. She had to tell about her day in first grade. She had gotten a gold star for being nice to her classmates. Angela hugged her mother's leg then looked up. Her bright blue eyes shined from her pale skin like two beacons in a dark night. She was the quiet one, but on this occasion her voice could be heard above everyone else's.

"Mommy! The kids at school said you were a failure."

The noise faded away.

"What did you say, darling?" her father asked.

"The kids said Mommy was a failure, that she couldn't catch the man that has been killing ladies," she said with her head tilted downward to the floor.

CJ put Harley down on the bed and knelt down in front of Angela. She gathered her into her arms and hugged her very tightly. She was crying openly. CJ wiped the tears from her eyes and tried to comfort her. She sat on the floor with Angela in her lap, rocking back and forth, saying, "It's all right. It's all right" again and again.

Finally, when Angela had quieted down, CJ talked with her. She explained that she and Lieutenant Hong were working hard to find the murderer, but it takes time to find evil men and women. She promised her that they would find and put the person in jail forever and ever. This seemed to satisfy her and she hugged and kissed her mother, but still wanted to sit in her mother's lap. Harley, who had started crying with her sister, came up and sat down on one of CJ's knees and hugged them both. Joel and his father sat down and the family huddled together on the bedroom floor.

CJ began to hum softly and she felt Angela snuggle up against her breasts. Harley edged her way under one arm, Joel under the other, and Rick, not to be left out, reached around them to encompass them

Racing though CJ's mind was what her daughter had said. Had they failed? Would the murderer go on murdering? She had to stop her. She had to draw her into the web she was weaving with Jim Hong. She had to find a way to bring justice for the women murdered.

The family stayed like that for an hour, CJ humming and rocking slowly. The light began to fail and Rick and CJ realized that all three children were asleep. They carried them to their beds and tucked them in for the night.

Returning to their own bedroom, they sat on the bed and talked into the early morning hours, saying things that they needed to say to each other. Both knew the danger and they discussed it openly. Rick knew she had to do this and he accepted it. He still had his fears, but CJ eased them by promising not to do anything without thinking it out, and reassuring him that she would never be more than a few feet from the other detectives. They packed the clothes in bags and climbed into bed. They held each other and drifted off to sleep.

It was a long day for Hong. It took a lot of planning and coordination for a month-long undercover operation. The organization of the operation, locations, the placement of support people—it all had to be planned. He didn't leave the office until late in the evening and went directly home. He had trouble sleeping, tossing and turning until he got up and walked around the house. His mind was crowded with fears for CJ. There were still too many unknowns. Too many things could go wrong. Everything was still up in the air and Hong knew it only too well. He went back to bed but couldn't sleep. Dawn was fast approaching when he finally drifted off to sleep, only to be awakened minutes later by the alarm clock.

It was raining outside.

He showered, shaved, ate breakfast, brushed his teeth, and then picked up an umbrella and headed out the door to his car. He drove to the station and sat in his car, waiting for CJ to arrive.

~ ~ ~

The morning was dark and rainy on the windward side of the island, and CJ rose quietly from the bed and left without waking Rich. She wanted to think on the way into the station without having the memory of Rick haunting her. The worry he had had the night before was heavy on her heart. Yet she had a job to do and was going to do it no matter what. The rain was coming down heavy now. It was hard to see in front of her and she slowed down. Her cell phone began to ring. She glanced at the readout. It was Rick.

"Hello, hon. I didn't want to wake you this morning when I left."

"I wish you had. I wanted to kiss you goodbye and wish you luck," he said.

"I know. I just had to leave, honey. I promise to take care of myself and will see you in a few days." She hung up the cell. The rain was pounding against the roof of the car as she started into downtown Honolulu. She sat in the car for several minutes, letting the rain ease her mind. Heavy rain always relaxed her. She was lost in her dream world when Jim tapped on the window and then slid into the passenger seat.

He quietly listened to the rain pattering against the roof and windshield. They sat there, not speaking, yet saying a million words. He had his fears racing through his mind and she had her concerns about her family.

Without looking at Jim, she said, "You know, I was going to resign this week."

"Yup," he answered, still looking straight ahead.

"Still may when this is over."

"You got the right."

Neither of them looked at the other, just stared straight ahead. Maybe it was because they couldn't look at each other at that moment. When two people were partners for so long, they know what the other was going to do without asking. They thought as one.

She reached across, took his hand, and squeezed it hard. She had never done that before and Jim looked down at her tiny hand that was pressing his with such force. He realized just how close they were as partners at that moment.

The rain let up and they went into the station.

~~~

John Morris had just risen from a restless night. He stood at the window and watched the rain sweep in from the ocean. It was creeping toward the shore, blotting out the ocean behind it; a wall of rain lashing at the shore headed for his window. He watched as it struck the shore and then advanced up the hill toward his home. It left nothing visible behind it. The drops of rain began to rattle the glass in the picture window. It was like a thousand bullets hitting the glass and then he could see nothing but gray.

Amy was lying atop the sheets naked. Her clothes were strewn helter-skelter about the room. She had come home late and stripped as she headed for bed, tossing a piece here and there. John had not heard her when she came in. She had slipped into bed trying not to wake him.

She had been drinking; he could smell the alcohol. She didn't have many faults, but drinking was her biggest. She moaned and pushed herself up from the sheets, then rolled over and pulled them around her. It was always the same. She would get so drunk she had to take a cab home and then pass out in the bed, sometimes fully clothed. The next day she would lay in bed until afternoon before coming downstairs, sunglasses on and very little else.

He walked away from the window and down the stairs to the kitchen. He sat down. He was waiting for a phone call and instructions on what he was to do at his office today. He had promised he would work with them closely but now he was having his doubts. He was afraid of what might happen. People had died because of him and he couldn't handle that. He made coffee, strong and hot. He could smell it as it brewed. The strong Hawaiian coffee aroma penetrated the house. He poured a cup and stood drinking it by the counter when she stumbled in, didn't say a word, poured a cup, and stumbled back up the stairs. He watched her moving from side to side going up the staircase. She wouldn't be down for hours.

The telephone rang. He answered it.

"Mr. Morris, are you going to be in your office this morning?" It was detective Hong.

"Yes."

"We'll see you there."

Morris hung up the phone and went upstairs to change into his work clothes while his wife lay sprawled across the bed. The gown she had worn downstairs was half on, half off her body. Morris peered at her creamy, silk thighs and felt aroused. Finishing buttoning his shirt, he left her behind and drove to work. He may have left her physically behind, but his memory was filled with her.

~~~

In Lanikai, Albert Kong was rising from a restless night. He knew that Dixie, his wife, had talked to the police, however, if he talked to her about it, she would know he was tapping her telephone and he didn't want that. He would have to let it go. She hadn't told them anything that could hurt him; in fact, she had actually helped him. A cripple couldn't possibly have committed the murders. Someone would have had to wheel him into the room, and that was ridiculous.

He looked at her uncovered back and bright red hair tumbling down and smiled. She might have called the cops, or had the cops call her, but she was still his woman and he wasn't going to harm her in any way. He put his arm around her and she rolled into him. They kissed deeply and passionately, locked in an embrace. She crawled on top and felt him slide into her. She leaned back and took complete control of their loving. She always enjoyed having control.

~~~

Charlie Kelly also was getting up early in the morning. He was headed for the *Daily*'s offices on King Street. He had a story that was going to put Hong and Jones on their butts. He was sure he knew who had done the killing and he was going to spill the beans in his column. It had to be Kong, or if not Kong, it had to be one of his henchman. The only thing that worried Kelly was, why? He hadn't figure that part out yet.

One thing about Kelly—he was cheap, as cheap as they come. He always rode Da Bus to and from work. The truth was he didn't own a car. He only used the newspaper's car when he went out on assignment. Today he had already reserved it for his venture to the police station for the 10 a.m. briefing by Chief Lester Streeter. He had his questions ready and was loaded for bear.

He hopped off the bus in front of the *Daily* Building and jogged up the stairs. The *Daily* Building was a structure out of the past. It was four stories high with the news offices on the second and third floors. The fourth floor held the office of the publisher and heads of various departments. The first floor was where the presses were. The building had been in the Kanahele family for over one hundred years. *The Daily* had its modest beginnings in early in the 1900s and grew to be the top newspaper in the island under the direction of Thomas Kanahele, Sam Kanahele's grandfather. The Kanahele's had simply followed one after the other in an unending line of top-notch journalists, battling for the rights of the native Hawaiians.

Kelly was whistling a little tune as he plopped down in his chair, turned on the computer, and waited for it finish its cycle so he could begin. When the chief read his column this morning there would be some interesting responses at the briefing.

The computer finished and Kelly began. His fingers sprang across the keyboard and the words lit up on the screen. Pausing after the first two paragraphs, he smiled. He had Hong and Jones right where he wanted them—directly behind the eight ball.

The sentence read "Albert Kong, underworld kingpin, both planned and executed the recent murders in what is being called the 'Murder By E-mail' case by the police. It is a fact, however, that the two officers in charge of the investigation ignored the facts and allowed a fourth murder to take place. The two officers, Lieutenant James Hong and Detective Sergeant Connie Jones are therefore responsible for the death of the fourth woman." He knew it could be slanted if he didn't have the proof to back it, and Kelly thought he had it; more than enough in fact to hang both detectives. He kept on smiling as he pounded away at the keys. The rain had begun to fall outside and he glanced out the window. *It's going to be a wet one,* he thought.

~ ~ ~

Captain Les Streeter woke with a head cold. He hated this weather. It always made him feel terrible. He rose, cleaned up, dressed, and found that his wife, Ruth, was up preparing breakfast for him.

"I tried not to wake you."

"I know, hon, but I can feel when you are not in the bed with me. I feel kinda lonely inside." She kissed him on the cheek while finishing his scrambled eggs. Bacon and toast were already on the table along with hot coffee—his usual breakfast. He sat down and between bites he sneezed and wheezed the breakfast morning away.

"Maybe you need to stay home today," she said, looking at him with concern.

"Can't, hon. I have to be there, big press conference today. Don't worry, I'll take care."

She nodded in agreement but was thinking, *Sure you will. You'll probably stand out in the pouring rain and catch your death of cold.*

He finished his meal, kissed her goodbye, and tossed on his raincoat as he left the house. Ruth cleared the dishes and washed everything before going back to bed for another hour. The rain was coming down harder now and she pulled the covers up around her chin and went back to sleep.

~~~

Miss Diane Puanani was still in bed. She wasn't asleep; she hadn't been since the first boom of thunder had shaken her awake. She was still thinking about the police and Mr. Morris. Yes, she was in love with John and had been for more than a year. Her nights were filled with him. She wore the most revealing clothes to work and had gone out of her way to show him a little leg or bare a part of her breast when she bent over him to discuss something, anything. He did not seem to notice. The day the police showed up she was about to throw herself at him and take whatever he would give her. She no longer cared if it meant her job. She needed him badly. Her desires were running wild in her body.

She lay in the bed listening to the rain patter against the windows. Today! Today she would come out and reveal her love for him. She knew that Amy was treating him like her bitch: always demanding and never thinking about him, only herself. She had watched how she had made love to him in his chair. She had cracked the door slightly and watched, wishing it were her who could be there making love to John. She felt a warmth deep in her belly and wanted him right that minute.

The alarm shattered her dream world, bringing her back to reality. *Today is the day*, she said again to herself, getting out of bed. She slipped out of her nightgown, the one she had purchased for herself when she had purchased another gift for Amy, as John had requested her to do. Her gift to herself, she imagined, to be worn when she made love to John. She gently lay it on the bed and showered.

She felt that today required special clothes. She toweled off, opened the bottom bureau drawer, and took out a golden colored box. She opened it and looked inside. She had spent two weeks of her salary for it, but it was what she wanted to hit him with when he arrived at the office. Before her was a silk dress, low cut but not too low, something acceptable for the office. She already had decided not to wear any panties or bra. She was going all out to seduce him today.

She put it on and looked at her reflection in the windowpane. She liked what she saw. She would have him today. The rain increased in tempo.

~~~

Captain Streeter had read the column in his office behind closed doors, but you could still hear him explode. He called for Hong and Jones. Streeter closed the door behind them and sat on the edge of his desk.

"Well, what are we going to do?"

"He hasn't got a thing. He's on a fishing expedition. If he knows something, then he was a fly on the wall when one of the murders happened," Hong said.

Streeter looked at Jones. She was rather quiet, considering it was Kelly they were talking about. She glanced up and caught Streeter's eyes.

"Nothing to say really," was her only commit.

"Okay then, time for the briefing. Either of you want to say anything?" Since they did not reply Streeter took that as a no.

The ten a.m. briefing was more like a miniature war. Everyone had read Kelly's breaking story. Some were angry, some were in disbelief, and others were just, well, shaking their heads, knowing Kelly had gone off half-cocked, like he usually did.

Streeter was more a fireman than a police officer as he tried to control the blaze that Kelly had lit. He answered question after question, sometimes with the total truth, other times simply setting it aside or avoiding it all together.

The briefing came to a complete halt as Kelly asked a question.

"Captain Streeter. Why is it that Hong and Jones are still on the case after letting the last woman be murdered?"

Every eye in the room was on Kelly and then Streeter. Streeter shifted his weight from one foot to the other before holding on to the podium with both hands and speaking clearly into the microphone.

"Mr. Kelly. Lieutenant Hong and Sergeant Jones have distinguished themselves on the Honolulu police force during their entire careers. To make an accusation of that nature without proof is very serious. If you have evidence, bring it to the authorities so we can investigate it and do the proper thing."

Now everyone was staring at Kelly waiting for his reply.

"I can't reveal my sources. If I show you the evidence, I would reveal the source. I can't do that. I will tell you that my source is placed very high in the state government. It is a very reliable source."

Heads were shaking. The other reporters knew he had nothing. He was just looking for a rise from one of the officers at the briefing. Streeter shifted his weight again and peered out at Kelly. Kelly sat down. The briefing was finished and the reporters broke up to return to their various newspapers, radio and television stations. The only one left was Kelly, still sitting in his chair. Jones took a step toward him and he was out the door.

~ ~ ~

Diane Puanani arrived early at the office. She made coffee. She had been planning what she was about to do all the way in. Her heart was pounding and she thought the people on the bus could hear it. She hadn't taken her car because her plans didn't including going home alone. She took a momentary look at the clock on her desk. Mr. Morris was late. He was never late. She began to worry. Would all her plans disappear because he was late and wouldn't have the time to see her? She wouldn't let that happen. This was her day, her night with him. At least once, she was going to possess him. She had to have him.

The door swung open and John Morris burst into the office, past Miss Puanani and into his office without saying a word to her. She was so taken back she didn't say a word. Her plans were crushed in that one second. She sat at her desk. At that moment she felt that her only hope would be for him to call her into his office or for her to find an excuse to go in and talk with him. But she had nothing. Plans and dreams were crumpling. She was about to die when Morris stuck his head out the door and called to her.

It was now. She glided into his office, up to his desk and made her play. He gazed up to see Diane's face inches from his own. She laced her arms around his neck and began passionately kissing him. At first he began to kiss her back, sharing the passion she was giving him. Then he began to struggle, pushing her away.

"Stop! Stop, damn it!"

He looked at her, stood up, and turned to the window, his head in his hands.

"John you can't reject me; I'm in love with you. I have been in love with you since that very first day, when you hired me. Can't you see it? I want you." She was behind him and put her arms around his waist, placing her head in the middle of his back. He unlocked her arms and stepped closer to the window. She placed her hands on her hips and took a deep breath.

"She's no good for you. She's ruined you; destroyed everything that makes you a man. I have watched it happen and died inside. I love you, John. I'll do anything you want me to do. I can make you the man you once were and make us happy."

Without turning, John said quietly, "Diane, I am married and that is all there is to it. I know how you feel, but other things besides the marriage are happening. People are dying because of me. You could be next on whatever list the mad man has."

"I don't care. You mean everything to me. Your wife doesn't care about you. I have seen it. She only cares about what she can get from you. Look at your life, John! She takes advantage of you, treats you like dirt one minute and then is all lovey-dovey the next, only because she wants something. I admit in the beginning she was there every step of the way, but not lately. It's now always me, me, me. John, you have to see what is really happening!"

John knew she was right; lately it had been about Amy all the time. He felt the pain and anger in his heart. She was right. He turned toward her, pulling her into his embrace. They were kissing again, long, hard, fulfilling their desires. Diane was rubbing against him. He could feel every curve of her young, tender body. His hand resting on her breast, he could sense her nipple becoming erect through the silky material.

She was just beginning to feel her success when the phone rang on his desk. He broke it off and reached for the phone. She continued to hold on to him her body pressed against him, searching for him to return to her.

"Hello?"

"Honey, it's me. Sorry about this morning and about not being home last night. Do you forgive me?"

"Of course."

"Be home early tonight! I'll be waiting for you with open arms. Love you."

"Same here."

He hung up the phone and returned his attention to Diane. Pushing her back onto his desk, he pulled her skirt up and found her naked. She reached down and removed his manhood from his pants; they made love on his desk.

She had won her battle for possession.

~~~

It was afternoon before Hong and Jones headed for the undercover location. The moving van was already there and the crew was unloading the furniture. They drove past the location to the place where Jones's car was waiting. She got out and Hong stopped her.

"You be careful, you hear!"

She nodded and went to the car, got in behind the wheel, and drove to the apartment. When she arrived, she directed the remaining unloading and set up inside. The men making the delivery were not police officers and knew nothing about what was happening. They were simply doing a job.

The apartment was a two-bedroom with a view of the mountains. The living room was large enough to seat a dozen or more people and the dining room had a table with seating for ten. In one corner was a computer, set up and ready to be used. She went to the bedroom, made the bed, took her personal items to the bathroom, and brewed coffee in the kitchen before making a tour of the rest of the house. The second bedroom had a bed and dresser and a small lanai that looked out over the mountains. She opened the door to the lanai and found a nice breeze blowing. She stood for several minutes enjoying it before going in, closing and locking the door. There was small utility room off the kitchen with a stacked washer and dryer. The final room was a den. A sofa and love seat were the primary seating items. There also were bookshelves on two walls. It was a very nice apartment set in a very well-to-do neighborhood.

After he mini-tour, she repeated it, only this time looking for the hidden cameras and mikes that the surveillance team had put into place the day before. She found all of them before she returned to the dining room and the computer.

She sat down and started the computer. It cycled through and she typed in her password, went to John Morris's name, and typed in her greeting. She saw his response. Pulling an opening script from her purse, she began to type.

This was the hardest part for her because what she was saying was not what she was like. Morris responded. She found that Morris had a very keen imagination when it came to sex. She found it hard to respond to some of the questions he posed to her. It made her almost sick to her stomach. She had never said any of the things she was saying to Morris, not even to her husband Rick.

Not that she was "Little Miss Innocent," but this was a little overboard for her. She thought about the moments with Rick in bed, and how they felt about their love-making. Those were true romantic moments. What she was typing was porno. They messaged back-and-forth for a half-hour before signing-off with a promise to meet again same time tomorrow.

She felt dirty when she finished and wanted to shower. Walking to the bedroom, she put her clothes away and started to unbutton her blouse. She was about to slip it off when she heard a voice over one of the speakers.

"I wouldn't do that. You do know you have an audience." It was Lieutenant Hong.

"Oh, yes, I forgot for a moment. Thanks for reminding me."

Hong was there, protecting her from her own mistakes. She gathered up what she was going to change into and headed for the bathroom, stopping to give one of the cameras a wink. This was the only show the guys were going to get from her.

In the bathroom, she slipped out of her blouse, skirt, and bra and then got into her pajamas and cover-up. She looked in the mirror and went to the living room. She picked up a copy of *Hawaii Today* and flipped the pages without reading it. Her first day undercover was coming to a close. The stage was finally set and now all she had to do was wait. Wait for what was coming. She walked to the window and stared out at the mountains. They were covered with lights from the houses, making it appears as if strings of Christmas tree lights covered it from top to bottom. It was going to be a long night. She knew it would be hard to sleep. Not being with Rick was one thing, but her mind was going to be listening for any strange noise or sound. It was too early for anything to happen, but still she couldn't stop thinking about where she was and what could happen. She stayed up until after midnight before going to bed.

~~~

John Morris finished working late but didn't go home that night. He went with Diane for a drink, which turned into love-making in her bed. He hadn't had such an enjoyable night in a long time. She treated him like a god. She anticipated his every desire and fulfilled it. She praised his love-making like he had never been praised before. When he finally decided to leave, she begged him to stay, but finally gave in to his wishes. They kissed at the door and he got into his car and left. It was 3 a.m.

All the way home he knew she would be waiting for him. It was all right for her to come in at 5 a.m., but he had to be home early. He knew for sure that Diane was right; Amy was using him for her own greedy desires and wants. He decided to have it out with her when he came through the door.

This was going to be the end of one relationship but the beginning of a new and wonderful relationship with Diane.

The hour to drive home gave him time to think about what he would say and do. As he pulled into the driveway he could see the house ablaze with lights. She was waiting. He stopped the car and sat for a moment, gathering all the strength he had for the battle set to begin. He got out of the car, walked to the front door, and was about to put the key into the lock when the door flew open and she stood there defiant, hands on hips, and a look that would rip the heart out of a live bird.

"Where the hell have you been?"

He looked at her and summoned up his nerve. "Away from you!"

"And what does that mean?"

"It means that I want a divorce," he blurted out.

She was stunned. John pushed her aside as he headed for the staircase to the bedroom. He was halfway up when he heard a crash and turned to see the remains of a large vase on the floor next to the door.

"You son-of-a-bitch!" she screamed. "You no good bastard, after all I have done for you. I gave up a career to marry you."

"Hell, you saw money and that's why you married me."

"You know that's a lie. You know that." She started to cry.

John was still midway up the stairs. He felt a twinge of pain for her. He had loved her deeply, but things had changed over the years. He started down and then stopped. She had this done this before and he had caved when she did it. *Not this time, not this time,* he said to himself and turned and leaped up the stairs to the bedroom.

He opened the closet, took down a suitcase, and tossed clothes in it. He heard her at the door. She was no longer crying. It had been a fake; she wasn't crying at all. He turned; she was gazing at him like a cat looking at its prey. He had seen that look before and knew what it meant.

She was planning something and she would destroy anything that got in her way.

"It's that bitch Diane, isn't it?"

"And if it was?"

"I'll get you back. No one takes anything away from me. I'll make her give you up. You hear me?"

"You leave Diane alone. If anything happens to her, I'll kill you."

There was silence. John had never spoken like that before to Amy.

He closed his bag and walked by her. He could feel her eyes burning into his back as he walked down the stairs. He flipped open the door and was out.

The sky had just a hint of daylight in it. He could see the streaks of light just breaking through the darkness, like fingers tearing away the sleepy night. He drove down the hill, turned onto the main highway, and headed back to Honolulu and into the welcoming arms of Diane.

~~~

Dixie was already out of bed and had showered, gotten into her bikini, and was drinking coffee on the lanai overlooking Lanikai Bay. She always loved the early morning. It made her feel good inside. She was watching the same morning sky as John Morris and enjoying it, but for a different reason. Albert and she were going on a trip to Kauai. They were going to a little cottage in the mountains for a weekend. She already had them packed and was just waiting for him to rise. He was always a late sleeper. She lit a cigarette, took a long drag, and then blew out the bluish colored smoke. She watched it float up and away as the stars faded and the sun took their place.

She hadn't told the detectives everything when they talked. She hadn't told them about her time with John Morris. John had contacted her online too. She had enjoyed their meetings. What would the police do if they knew she had a long-time relationship with a man that was at the top of their list of murder suspects? Dixie knew more than she was telling. She crushed out her cigarette and stood up. It was time for her morning swim in the pool. She plunged into the cold water and did several laps before pulling herself out. Her body was chilled and her breasts were firm under the bikini bra, her erect nipples clearly visible. She toweled off and walked back into the house. She hadn't noticed Albert watching her from the bedroom window.

Albert had his mind on what the day was about to offer and he smiled. He knew more than he was telling. He knew about Dixie's relationship with Morris. He knew they had spent an hour on the net having cyber sex. He knew she had stopped the relationship. He knew it all. He loved her and cared about her very much and that was the only thing he cared about. Everything was going to work out. He had already set into motion his own plans for Mr. Morris.

~~~

Like John, Diane had stayed up after he left. She had remained awake, dreaming of what would happen next. John had said he was going to tell Amy that he wanted a divorce. She was sitting on the lanai enjoying the early morning as the sun was rising. She was still in her nightgown drinking in the first morning rays of light when John's car appeared in the driveway. She saw him step out and sprang to her feet, leaping down the steps and into his waiting arms. Their kiss was long and passionate. Deep in each other's soul it went. When they finally parted there was a torrid fire burning in both of them. They didn't speak a word, only dashed up the stairs and into Diane's bedroom to complete their desires.

John lowered her slowly onto the bed, kissing her passionately again, drawing her love from her body. She melted into him and in moments they were locked together on the bed, making love as they had the evening before. The sunlight reached into the room, adding its warmth to the already passionate couple devouring each other in the morning light.

~~~

Lieutenant Hong had not left the apartment beside CJ's. He had lain down and rested on a sofa, but he wouldn't leave. Detective Dan Tow was sitting watching a camera shot of CJ's living room, focused on the computer area. It had been a very quiet evening.

CJ came out of the bedroom and winked at the camera. Tow laughed, waking Hong from his sleep.

"What?"

"Nothing boss, just CJ winking at the camera this morning. She's dressed for work already. Nice outfit if I do say so myself."

"Dan, you're here to keep her safe, not judge her wardrobe."

"Yes sir."

CJ was headed for her "job" at the real estate office in Waikiki. It was all part of the planned undercover operation. Only the owner knew who CJ really was and of course, the owner would be handling any of the business deals for her. CJ was going to be a window piece in case the murderer stalked the victim before killing her. She signaled she was leaving and closed the door behind her.

The outside detail already had her in sight as she got into her car and headed for Waikiki. She glanced in the rear view mirror and saw the officers behind her. They tailed her all the way to the real estate office and when she pulled in they parked across the street and waited.

CJ went to her office and turned on the computer. She was waiting for John to come online. Her duties were light all day and it gave her time to send and receive messages from him. When he first called her, there seemed to be something strange about the conversion. There were gaps in his thoughts, incomplete messages and ideas. CJ wasn't sure about what was happening, but she continued to chat, hoping to better understand him. They chatted for over an hour before signing off, with a promise to meet that night online for some cyber sex. The last part of the messaging seemed to be more in line with what they had been planning to say.

After hanging up, CJ called Lieutenant Hong and told him about what she was feeling about the call. It didn't seem right and Hong agreed; there was something amiss. He left the stakeout and headed for Morris's office.

When Hong got to the office, he found the reception room vacant. He looked around for Miss Puanani but she was nowhere to be found. He headed for Morris's office. As he swung the door open, he spied them locked in each other's arms passionately kissing. Hong closed the door quietly and then knocked on it before reentering.

"Am I interrupting anything?" he asked coming through the door.

"No, just talking with Diane—I mean Miss Puanani. Thank you! We'll finish later," he said as Miss Puanani left through the door Hong had just come in.

Yes, thought Hong, *I am sure you will finish later.*

"Mr. Morris, I just talked with Detective Jones and she is concerned about your messaging today."

"I called her just like I said I would and we chatted."

"Yes, I know, but it was how you chatted. You acted as if your mind was a million miles from the conversation. You have to stay with the script we have devised if we are to catch the person behind the murders. Everything you do affects the situation that Detective Jones is in. I will not allow you or anyone else to put her in jeopardy. You got that, Mr. Morris?"

"Yes, I understand. I understand very well."

"If anything happens to my partner, I would suggest you leave town, change your name and appearance, because I will come for you."

"Are you threatening me?"

"No. Just making a statement of fact."

Their eyes met. It was a long hard stare before Hong broke it.

"Mr. Morris, just what is going on with your secretary?"

"Lieutenant, that has nothing to do with you!"

"I am afraid you are wrong. Anything that you do affects what is happening on the stakeout and I need to know what is happening."

Morris looked at him, turned, and sat down behind his desk. He opened up by telling Hong about what had happened the night before, including his rendezvous with Diane, the fight at his house, and what he had told Amy. He went on to tell about his plans after he was divorced, which included Diane.

This was more than Hong had bargained for. CJ had figured that there were three women that could be involved with the murders, Dixie Kong, Miss Diane Puanani and Mrs. Amy Morris. Any one of them could be triggered by anything that Morris did, and CJ would find herself in very deep trouble. Dixie wanted to protect her husband at all costs, including covering up the fact that she, herself also talked with Morris. Diane wanted Morris for herself and might do anything to get him, including murder, and then there was the jealous wife, Amy, who would do anything to keep him. Besides the women, Hong had not left out Albert Kong as a possible murderer. Hong was sure Kong knew about the affair with his wife, and revenge was a strong possibility. Too many suspects and not enough clues made Hong's head spin.

He gazed back into Morris's eyes again.

"Morris, I don't care! My only concern is my partner. Your life is already screwed up; just don't screw up someone else's." Hong turned for the door.

"And get this straight: stay with the program. We need to catch the murderer!" He slammed the door as he left.

Morris sat behind his desk, dropped his head into his hands, and began to weep softly. Hong was right and he knew it. If it was one of the ladies, then everyone was in jeopardy. He heard the door open and looked up. Diane was standing there. She had listened through the door and now knew she had to be with Morris. He needed her and she wasn't afraid of anything. She walked over to him. He stood up, and she put her arms around his neck and kissed him.

"I love you, honey. I'll always be here for you, no matter what happens." She kissed him again and he responded.

~~~

The day ended for CJ with her signing off to John and going to her car. She glanced across the street and saw the undercover officers watching her. She drove home knowing they were behind her. She stopped at a convenience store at the bottom of the hill before heading up to her apartment. She picked up some odds and ends and packed them into the front seat. She was turning around when she felt someone very close to her. Her police instincts made her move her hand toward her concealed pistol. She was ready, but then she heard the person move on by and into the store. The night air was filled with the stench of beer; he was a drunk looking for more beer. She breathed a little easier, stood up, and leaned against the car. The undercover officers were getting back into their vehicle. CJ gave them a simple nod and went around to get in her own vehicle. She slid behind the wheel, started the car and pulled out into traffic. It took only minutes to arrive at the apartment, where she carried her small grocery bag up to the apartment and went in.

After unloading the groceries, she took a shower, changed into her nightclothes, and turned on the computer. John was to be waiting for her, and he was. They chatted for an hour before signing off. CJ still was having trouble with the words and descriptions that they were using with each other, but if they were to catch the murderer, she would have to carry out the deception.

She stood by the window and gazed out at the falling night, wishing she could be home with her children and later climb into bed with her husband in Kaneohe instead of sleeping by herself in an apartment filled with microphones and cameras. She longed for her husband's arms around her and his warm kiss on her lips. She went to the telephone and was going to call him but stopped. It would be out of place to do something like that, so she backed off and sat down to watch some television. It was going to be a long stakeout.

Around midnight, she got up and went to bed, ending an unproductive day and an even more unproductive evening.

~ ~ ~

Amy Morris had left the house in the morning and had not returned. She drove around the island, stopping at several places to try and blow off some steam. She wasn't happy any more and she was going to destroy Diane. She didn't care about anything else. She had to get rid of Diane. She was sitting on a park bench near Ala Moana Center, when she decided to go the John's office and confront Diane and have it out, even if it meant killing the bitch. The trip to the office took only minutes. She pulled into the parking area and saw John's and Diane's cars parked side-by-side. She started a slow burn. All the energy she had used up and gotten rid of returned in a matter of moments. She flung open the car door and rushed up to the office. She burst into the outer office and slammed open John's office door.

Standing in the middle of the office were John and Diane, locked in each other's arms in a deep passionate kiss.

"You fucking little bitch!" Amy screamed as she leaped at the pair, grabbing Diane by the hair and pulling her to the floor in a heap beside the desk. She had Diane's hair in one hand and was slapping her with the other as they rolled around on the floor. Diane, at first startled, began to fight back. John was trying to separate them. The pair were kicking and clawing at one another, and it took several minutes for him to finally get between them and hold them apart.

Amy was like a wild animal, breathing hard, fire in her eyes, her blouse torn and blood trickling down from her lip. Diane was none the less for wear. Her dress was torn in the front, revealing her bare breasts. Her hair was in total disarray and there was blood running from her nose. She covered herself as best she could as she stared at her opponent. John placed himself between the pair after watching the cat fight in his office.

"Amy, I told you it was over between us and I meant it. It is over. Get out of here or I will call the cops."

"No little whore is going to steal from me. You're mine and always will be. Please, John! I love you."

"No, Amy; it's done. It has been for months now, only I didn't know it. I figured we could make it right, but we can't. I don't love you any more. I don't care about you any more. Leave now, or I will call the police." He moved to the desk and picked up the phone.

"You'll be sorry. You both will be sorry. I'll leave but you will never be rid of me! Never! And you, you bitch—you will regret the day you crossed my path." She turned and flew out of the office.

John helped Diane into his chair and got a cloth to stop the bleeding from her nose. He took his coat, covered her up, and then knelt beside her, holding her hand. She was crying, sobbing softly. He had never seen her cry, and it was tearing him apart. He kissed her forehead and gathered her up into his arms. She pressed her head against his shoulder and snuggled close. It was so warm and relaxing in his arms. She closed her eyes and wrapped her arms around him. It was good to feel safe warm in the arms of the man you love. Morris picked up the telephone, called Lieutenant Hong, and told him about the incident. Hong asked if Miss Puanani wanted to press charges of assault. Morris asked. She shook her head no and Morris told Hong. Morris hung up the phone.

Amy had stormed out of the building, rushed to her car, and had driven away like a maniac. She sped onto the highway, forcing cars off the road as she weaved in and out of traffic. She pounded the steering wheel as she raced along, fleeing the Waikiki area and bolting onto the freeway. She headed for Hawaii Kai and then onto Kalanioneohe Highway, finally pulling over at Makapuu Beach Park. She slumped over and rested her head on the wheel; tears were streaming down her face and the anger in her was boiling over. She hated both John and Diane, yet she wanted John back. He was hers and no one was going to take him away. She would get him back, but before she got rid of Diane, she had one other thing she would have to do. One last item to make sure John was hers and hers alone.

She looked at herself in the rearview mirror. She needed to repair the damage her crying had done before she finished her work for the day. She wiped and cleaned her face then reapplied her makeup. She looked again and was pleased. *See?* she thought, *No one can hurt me, and no one could take anything from me*. She was the most beautiful woman on the islands; John would realize that and come running to her once Diane was out of the picture.

She started the car and headed back into Honolulu. She had a job to do, a last item before she could take care of Diane and take possession of John. The return drive back was slow because she needed it to be dark when she arrived back at John's office. She needed it to be empty. She had something to do and she needed to do it alone.

~ ~ ~

Kong was sitting in a chair by the pool, waiting for Dixie to come down. Everything was ready for the trip. Across from the poolside table sat Mike Patrick. He had just arrived from the mainland. He had flown in by request of Mr. Kong. They were talking low so no one could hear them.

Kong had set up a contract on John Morris, on the man that had fooled with his wife. Kong was serious about the hit and had offered a hundred thousand dollars. It couldn't be a gangland style hit; it had to look like an accident. So Patrick was called on. Known in the underworld as Mr. Accident, Mike Patrick would take down anyone—for a price, that is.

"I don't want to know when, where, or how, as long as it is a clean hit. You got that, Mike?"

"Yes sir, Mr. Kong. It won't be a problem.
"Good."
Patrick stood up and turned to leave, when Dixie appeared in the doorway to the swimming pool.
"Leaving so soon, Mr.—I didn't get the name?"
"Mike, Mike Peters. It's nice to meet you, Mrs. Kong. I have to be going. I'm afraid I have some work to do in Honolulu before flying home. It was nice seeing you again, Mr. Kong, and nice meeting you, Mrs. Kong." He gave a slight bow and was gone.

Dixie watched him go then turned to Albert.
"Why is he here?"
"He just came by to pay his respects; that's all."

She looked at him and could tell he was lying. She looked away and sipped her drink. He went back to the newspaper he had in front of him. He flipped it up and glanced at the front-page headlines. Nothing of importance was on the front but as he skimmed the pages, he saw a headline in the editorial page that pulled him into the story.

As he read the story his face changed. It appeared that Mr. Kelly had been doing some more digging and was going to do some more finger-pointing. Kong didn't know whether to believe what he had just read or let it go as Kelly being his stupid self again. The article stated that Kelly had gotten firsthand information about the killer and was going to announce the killer in his column tomorrow. Kong remembered when he had pulled the same stunt a few days back and had been blasted by the chief of police. Then he paused and thought again. Kelly would never try the same trick twice; maybe he had something this time. Kong signaled for the houseboy to bring a telephone. He needed to contact Mr. Kelly.

Kelly was at his desk when the receptionist announced he had a call. He picked up the phone and answered.
"Good morning, Mr. Kelly."
Kelly knew the voice; it was Albert Kong.
"Good morning, Mr. Kong. What can I do for you?"
"I don't know. Maybe it is what we can do for each other?"

In the next ten minutes they exchanged information and Kelly was recording the conversation so he could play it back and draw out every detail. Kong told him about the interview with Hong and CJ. Kelly provided the meager information he had on the case. When all was said and done, Kong knew that Kelly was running a bluff. Kelly didn't know the murderer, nor who would be the next victim, but Kong knew where there was a detective sergeant that was using herself as bait. This he didn't tell Kelly.

After they hung up, Kong stared out at the pounding surf and laughed. Kelly knew absolutely nothing. Wouldn't he be surprised when one of the prime suspects came up dead! John Morris was going to have an accident. Kong suddenly felt as if someone was staring at him, and he was right. Dixie had affixed her eyes on the back of his head. He turned and met her eye-to-eye. Her stare was intense, burning into his face. He found it hard to look at her.

"I want the truth, Albert. The whole truth, none of your bullshit. Why is Mike Patrick here? He didn't come to pay his respects. He's here on a job and I want to know what that job is!"

Kong could never lie to her. She always knew when he was lying.

"He's here for a hit, baby."

"On who?"

There was a long silence as Kong debated whether to tell her or not. When his eyes met hers he knew there was nothing he could do but tell the truth.

"John Morris."

She stood up; a look of disbelief spread cross her face.

"Why?"

"You know why! He is the cause of all the murders and you and he have had a relationship via messaging. You could be the next victim. I think he is doing the killing and the police don't realize they are actually working with the murderer."

"You idiot. He is only one end of it. He isn't the murderer; besides, I am in no danger. This place is like a fortress. Anyone trying to get in would be shot full of holes. Besides, a woman is doing the killing; I am sure of that."

There was an icy silence. Then, without another word, Dixie turned and walked back into the house. Albert watched as she went and as the door closed behind her, he resumed reading his newspaper.

~~~

CJ spent the morning at the office. It was quiet, as business was down at the moment. She messaged Morris twice in the morning and once in the afternoon, each time receiving highly sexual responses, as was pre-planned. It was late in the afternoon when Lieutenant Hong dropped by the office posing as a costumer and asked to speak to CJ. She met him at her office door and invited him inside. She closed the door and then sat down.

"How's it going?" Hong asked.

"Okay, I guess. Nothing out of the unusual, I would say."

"I have a feeling something is going to happen soon. Did you hear about the ruckus at Morris' office between his wife and secretary?"

"No, I didn't."

"Well, according to Morris, his wife flew into a rage and attacked his secretary. It turned into a real cat fight, with hair being pulled, clothes torn off, and bloody noses on both of them. Mrs. Morris left afterwards and was followed by an undercover officer." She drove out to Makapuu and then returned to Honolulu, where the officer lost her in traffic. We don't know where she is now."

"Jimmy, I think you'd better find her. You know she is the one, I think, who has been doing the killings. Morris's secretary could be in danger. She could be the next victim!"

"Already done, CJ, but we still have to be concerned about you as well. There is another problem that you should know about. Kong has hired a hit man from L.A., a Mr. Mike Patrick. He arrived yesterday and paid a visit to Kong this morning. I think he is here to take out Morris."

"You're kidding!"

"No, I'm not. I figure Kong found out that his wife was talking with Morris via messaging and he has decided to handle this his own way."

"Shit. This is getting out of hand. What are you planning on doing?"

"I have already put a plain-clothed man on him. Believe me, I know every move he has made. Now I want you to take care of yourself the next couple of days. I got a feeling all hell is about to break loose, and CJ, I want you to be especially careful in the apartment."

"I'll be fine. That apartment has more cameras than all the local TV stations combined. You guys know what I am doing 24/7, including when I go to the bathroom."

"Okay. I better be going."

"Let's make this look like you are just another local looking for property."

"By the way I used the name James Yamashiro when I came in."

She went to the door and opened it, stepped into the corridor, and pointed out several pictures of choice properties on the wall. Each one carried a price tag of several millions of dollars. They paused at one or two of the photos and Hong made the appearance of someone truly interested in purchasing as he scanned the data and asked several questions. They finally came to one near the main offices and CJ pointed it out.

"This would be perfect for your business, Mr. Yamashiro. The location is exactly what you need. The price is just right and we could get you into the offices in a matter of weeks and not months."

"Well, I'm not sure. I'll have to think about it. Thank you anyway, Miss Wineberger. I'll discuss it with my board and we will get in contact with you, one way or the other."

They shook hands. CJ escorted Hong to the front door and he departed.

"Do you think you can sell him on that property?" Vanessa Murakami asked from her office opposite the photo.

"Don't know, but he was interested," CJ replied.

~ ~ ~

That evening fell like a curtain on a bad play. It began to rain around six o'clock. It started as a light drizzle, but by seven it had increased to a torrent, pounding the windowpanes at Diane's house and making the night darker than usual. Diane was alone, waiting for John's arrival. She had gone home after the altercation with Amy and rested. John had said he would be coming later, sometime around eight or nine that evening.

Across town, CJ was waiting for John also, only she was waiting for his usual email messaging. As she sat at the computer, she could hear the rain splattering against her windows. The lights from her living room didn't seem to penetrate the darkness and she suddenly felt very alone. Glancing at the location of one of the hidden cameras, she felt a little better knowing her fellow officers were just next door, ready to come to her aid if she needed them.

She saw a message box appear. It was John. She responded and they went through the usual chatting. This time, however, there was something just a little different. Halfway through the messaging, John began to ask her to remove her clothing and sit nude in front of her computer. This was not in the usual routine. This was something that was never in the messages to the other women, at least not from Morris. CJ felt a cold chill run down her spine. Was this how the other women were lured into taking off their clothes before they were murdered? CJ was at a loss. Was the killer as well as the police watching her?

Then there was the problem of her clothes. Would the killer strike if she kept her clothes on? If CJ took off clothes to lure the murderer into the apartment, then her protectors became voyeurs. She typed a *"no"* in the message box and waited.

The cursor flashed but didn't move. Then the words *"Okay, but if you don't there won't be a surprise for your tonight"* danced across the screen. CJ replied with another *"no."* Again the cursor flashed but didn't move. CJ stared at the screen and waited. Then it moved again spelling out the words *"Okay, but I won't be back to you until tomorrow and you have to make up your mind if you want the surprise or not."*

CJ typed, *"Wait."*

But after several minutes there was no reply. Had the murderer visited her with the request for nudity before the murder? Or was John playing a new game?

Looking up into the hidden camera CJ spoke clearly. "I need to speak with Hong, now!"

"He just left the station, CJ. I called him when I saw the part about you getting naked. He's already on his way."

"Thanks."

Five minutes later Hong knocked on the door. CJ opened it.

"So what have we got?"

"I think someone patched into the chat tonight. I think it was the murderer asking me to take off my clothes. I said no, but according to that person if I wanted the surprise I would have to be naked tomorrow."

Hong looked at her. Sure all the other victims had been nude, but this was something they hadn't thought about.

"If I have to take my clothes off to bring the murderer to justice, I will, but I want some females doing the observing, not a bunch of over-sexed, under-loved, horny cops drooling on the TV monitors. Besides, knowing those idiots, they have already made photos of me in my night gown and those are all over the station."

Hong had already picked up the photos CJ was talking about and had changed the surveillance crew. Reprimands had been handed out to two of the former crew and they had been put on desk jobs for a month.

"Not a problem, CJ. In fact, three of the surveillance crew are women. I will replace the other one, tomorrow morning. Understand the assistance crew remains male. We don't really know if our killer is male or female. I have to protect you at all costs when it finally goes down."

"That's okay with me. Sorry to be such a bitch about this, but I have enough problems at the station house."

"It's not a problem, CJ. You know that."

Just then a bell rang on the computer. They looked at it. John was buzzing her. CJ answered.

"Sorry I am late tonight," came the words on the screen. CJ and Hong looked at one another. CJ had been visited by the murderer and would be visited again tomorrow night.

~~~

The next morning, Kelly was waiting for Hong at the police station. He was scared. The telephone call from Albert Kong was enough to scare anyone. Now the question was, would the police help him, protect him if they had to, and if he needed to be protected. Sure, he had been a pain in the butt for the force, but he had his reasons, and they weren't just about causing trouble for Hong.

Hong pulled up and parked his car. He had already seen Kelly at the front door waiting. Hong thought to himself it was probably just as well that Kelly was outside and not inside. There were several on the force who would like to take his head off. Hong waited in the car until Kelly finally started over. He knocked on the window and Hong rolled it down.

"Something I can do for you, Kelly?"

"Can we talk, Jimmy? I've got a problem and I need help, I think."

"Sure. Get in and we'll go for a ride."

Kelly shifted around to the other side of the vehicle and got it. Hong started car and pulled out of the parking lot and onto the highway, heading for the *Daily News* offices. They hadn't been on the road but a minute or so when Kelly began to speak.

"I got a telephone call from Albert Kong yesterday. He was asking me what I know about the murders you're investigating. I didn't tell him anything, but I think he thinks I know something and I'm afraid of what he might do."

"Well, Charlie, when you shoot off your mouth, sometimes it backfires!"

"Jimmy, you have to protect me!"

"Give me one good reason why I should, after all the problems you have caused on this investigation."

"Come on, Jimmy, I was just trying to do my job."

"Your job? Look Charlie, you stick your nose in where it isn't needed, you make up 'facts' and then when the hot water gets poured on you, you come looking for protection."

"Jimmy, I promise to never cause the force any more problems."

"If I could believe that I would, but unfortunately I don't."

There was silence in the car as they pulled into the *Daily*'s parking lot. Jimmy half turned in the car and looked at Kelly. Kelly was hanging his head and fear seemed to issue from every pore on his body. Hong felt sorry for the man, but then again, Kelly had gotten himself into this mess by printing his beliefs and not the facts.

"All right, I'll have an officer stationed at your home. I'll have to select someone because I don't think we could get a volunteer. He'll meet you here at the end of your work day, around four p.m."

"Thanks, Jimmy. You won't be sorry. I promise I will be a great help to the force from now on."

Kelly got out of the car and dashed up the staircase. Hong shook his head and laughed. He already knew about the phone call and just what Kong had asked and what had been said. It was nice to have an inside man at Kong's estate in Lanikai.

Hong headed back to the station.

~~~

John Morris was just waking up; beside him lay Diane. It had been another wonderful night with her. Their love-making had brought him to life for the first time in years. She was everything he had wanted when he had married Amy, and thought he was getting. Now he had more than he could have ever imagined. He leaned over and kissed Diane on the forehead and watched as she stirred from her sleep. She reached up and kissed him passionately. They fell back onto the bed and let their emotions carry them away. It was a warm feeling that swept over them, one both had been seeking and had at last found. They would be late for work again today.

~~~

Amy Morris had a fitful night, spending it at the beach park near Ala Moana. She was a mess. Hate filled her mind and it could be seen in her eyes. Revenge was the only thought she had. She would get her revenge soon and she could hardly wait for the moment.

~~~

Albert Hong and Dixie had not gone to the outer islands as planned. Dixie had refused to leave her room and she didn't care to talk with Albert. He had flown into a rage and everyone avoided him. Things had not changed from the day before. Dixie was in her room and Albert at the pool. It wasn't going to be a great day for anyone at the Kong estate.

~~~

CJ woke early, dressed, and was at work before the sun rose. She went through the routine as before, but her mind wasn't on anything but the coming evening. The day was spend uneasily waiting for the night and her "visitor" she felt would be coming. Several of the other employees in the office came by to say hello and chat about the everyday events of the office, but CJ only half paid attention. Her mind was already in the apartment at the computer, waiting for the events of the evening to unfold. She knew or at least she felt she knew, that tonight would be the conclusion of the case. She left the office at the usual time and returned to the apartment.

Lieutenant Hong was already at the apartment with the female officers of the surveillance team. He had decided that he would stay there until it went down and an arrest was made. He had a funny feeling inside that it would happen that evening, that all their hard work and effort were coming to a rapid and final end. Everything pointed to the case coming to a close. Things had been planned well and Hong was checking them over again to make sure everything and everyone was in place.

He saw CJ enter the apartment, turn on the computer, and go to the bedroom. She spoke softly into one of the microphones in the bed.

"Who's got the duty tonight?"

"Lieutenant Hong and officers Rose Carrey, Susan Miyasaki, and Trisha Chen are in the next room and I have the monitor duty. I am Janet Brison."

"Hi, Janet. I'll be changing into my bathrobe in a few minutes and then be sitting at the computer. Is everyone ready?"

"Yes everything is set. Lieutenant Hong and the other officers are waiting for my go when things start to go down. We have you covered, CJ."

"I hope so."

CJ began to change her clothes, removing everything and replacing them with just a bathrobe, which she intended to remove when she was sitting at the computer. She was still self-conscious and not comfortable with what was going to take place, but if they were going to catch the murderer, this would have to be what she would do. She opened the closet and selected the mid-thigh, blue, silk Chinese robe and walked into the living room. It took only seconds for the messaging to open and she looked at an empty screen. It appeared to be the beginning of a long night.

~~~

Mike Patrick was sitting in his hotel room cleaning his revolver. It was something he always did before a hit. He liked the feel of the cold steel in his hands. He had selected the piece at a local pawnshop. It was a 380 auto. It had been well kept and appeared almost new. The bluing on the weapon had only a mark. He usually used a 380 on all his hits. They were small, easy to handle, and up close, provided plenty of killing power. He began to reassemble the piece, checking the smoothness of the parts fitting together. When he finished, he checked the action of the weapon and trigger squeeze. It would do, he finally concluded, and placed it in the inside pocket of his jacket on the chair. He checked his watch. One hour before he would kill Morris and his mistress, and another two hours before he left for the mainland.

He had planned out the hit quickly, but he figured that he could do it, because neither of the victims knew they were being stalked. It would be easy and quick and he would be on his way home. He hated the long flights he had been taking lately, but there really wasn't a choice; a job was a job.

He lay down on the bed and closed his eyes. It was going to be a fast evening and he needed to be prepared.

~~~

Diane had prepared a dinner at the house, and she and John had enjoyed it by candlelight. They sat at the table, held hands, and simply stared into each other's eyes. Two people could not have been happier. John leaned across the table and kissed her. She kissed him back long and deep.

They were deeply in love and nothing would stand in their way. Their happiness was going to be first and foremost in their world. Neither said a word as he scooped her up into his arms and walked back to the bedroom. He laid her down on the bed, kissing her gently. He slowly removed her blouse as she tugged at his clothes, each kissing the other passionately. Their love was a fire burning deep in their bodies and souls. It was a passion, a desire to possess each other every second of every day. They felt warmth. They felt the fire burn and they made love as the sun set into the Pacific Ocean.

It was good to have such an intense love.

~ ~ ~

Kelly found comfort in the fact that outside his house was a Honolulu officer. Hong had come through for him and provided him with protection. He would have preferred several more officers, but one was good enough for the time being. He would rest a lot easier tonight. He sipped his coffee and watched a sitcom on TV. He was safe.

~ ~ ~

Amy was still at Ala Moana Park as evening was settling in. Her car was parked facing the ocean and she was watching the waves roll into the sandy beach. She hadn't moved from the spot since arriving early that morning. She was thinking about John and Diane and the hate she possessed was at the boiling point, ready to explode. Her eyes were on fire, red with anger and passion. She was filled with the desire for revenge. Revenge. Revenge was all that she was feeling. Death only would be the final outcome of her intense passion. Death to any and all that stood between her and John. She was going to deal it out tonight, death to Diane. It would be death to all John's lovers

~ ~ ~

Evening began to creep across the island like a cat on soft paws, moving between the palms, down the streets and byways into the lives of the islanders. Lights began to appear in the houses that lined the mountains overlooking Waikiki. The noises of the evening coming from the entertainment centers of Oahu echoed across the island. Hawaii was beginning another fun night. On the streets, people headed for their favorite restaurants or were sitting down to a home-cooked meal. Music filled the air and laughter livened up the early evening.

Tonight would be like any night in the islands. Some would find happiness, some loneliness. Others would fall in love and others would fall out of love. People would live and die. It would be like any major city in the United States; only here in Hawaii, the lives of everyone involved with the e-mail murders were about to collide head-on. Time was running out.

~~~

Mike Patrick woke when the telephone rang. He glanced at his watch. The desk was right on time with his wake up call. He sat up, answered, then rose and picked up his briefcase. He opened the door and found two plain-clothed officers and two HPD officers waiting for him. He started to make a move for his weapon but stopped. He knew there was no chance.

"Mr. Mike Patrick? Honolulu PD. You are under arrest for carrying a concealed weapon in the state of Hawaii without a permit."

The other plain-clothed officer read him his rights as the uniformed officers cuffed him and led him away.

"Jimmy had it pegged right to the last iota."

"Yeah, he is always good at making the pinch at the right time. Glad he is on our side." They both smiled and laughed.

Hong had set up the arrest almost as soon as he got the word from his agent in Kong's household. The man undercover there was a brave individual and Hong had the deepest respect for him. It had taken three years to plant him there, but it had been worth every minute since, as information flowed out of that house into the police station, helping to prevent a number of crimes and save lives.

John Morris was a lucky man. Mike Patrick never failed once he had taken a murder-for-hire contract. This would be a first time for the hired killer. The laws in Hawaii about carrying a concealed weapon were harsh. Mike Patrick was going to do time; there was little doubt of that.

~~~

John and Diane were still in bed wrapped in each other's arms when John was jerked away by the sound of breaking glass and the crash of someone breaking down a door. He reached for his pants and pulled his pistol from pocket, then rolled out of bed, waking Diane.

"Stay where you are! Someone is breaking into the house!"

He crept to the bedroom door and slowly opened it. In the light from the living room he could just make out a figure moving about. He yelled out "Freeze!" but was greeted with a shot that slammed into the doorframe, so he quickly slammed the door and locked it.

"Out the window, now!" he called to Diane and then watched as she slid out the window. He grabbed his pants and her dressing gown and tossed them out after her. Then he followed. He hit the ground beside her and struggled into his pants before they both ran toward the street.

Another shot rang out as they turned the corner. John paused and fired back at the figure. They continued to run down the street. John flagged down a passing police vehicle and told their story while panting. He then asked for Lieutenant Hong.

Ten minutes later they were in the Honolulu police station. Lieutenant Hong was informed by phone of the situation. He ordered that the pair be placed under protective custody. Patrol cars were sent to the house and a street-by-street search gotten underway. As for John and Diane, their night was over and they were safe.

~ ~ ~

Across the city in her apartment, CJ was still at the computer and the screen was still blank. She was still wearing her robe and waiting for the first message to come in. The minutes ticked away and she began to fidget in her chair. She was about to get up and make a cup of coffee when the message box appeared.

"Are you there?"

CJ typed slowly *"Yes, I am here."*

"Good. Are you naked?"

"No, but I can be in a minute. Wait!"

She stood up and slid the robe off her shoulders and let it drop to the floor. She sat down and began to type again. *"I am naked now."*

"You wouldn't lie to me, would you?"

"No, I am naked. Honestly, I am naked, like you asked. Why do you want me to be naked? We can't see each other?"

"You don't need to know why I want you naked! You only need to obey me."

"Yes, I will obey."

"Good! Now my surprise for you is something you have always wanted. Something you have desired for a long time. You have been trying to get it for a long time and now you will have it, only not the way you expected."

CJ sat waiting for the next message but it never came on the screen. Instead, it came from behind her.

A hand grabbed CJ's hair and pulled her from the chair. She reached for the hand that had grabbed her by the hair but she was cut by a knife. She blocked it from slicing her throat. CJ grabbed the assailant's arm, tossing the small-framed body over CJ's head to the floor. The figure dressed from head-to-toe in black slashed at CJ, who went into a defensive posture, protecting her body from the knife wielded by the assailant.

They circled each other and CJ stared at the blue eyes peering at her from the slits in the mask. She could feel the hatred pouring from the eyes. The assailant lunged and CJ grabbed the out-stretched arm and threw her to the floor. With the attacker lying on the floor and CJ on top, holding the knife hand, the detective was able to place a well-aimed fist into the masked face.

By the time Hong and the rest of the stakeout squad broke into the room, CJ had the situation well in hand.

The motionless body was handcuffed and Hong pulled the mask off. It was Amy Morris. Blood oozed from her lip, trickling down to her chin.

CJ was standing beside Hong looking down at the murderer.

"Well, you were right. It was a female."

"Yeah, I guessed it was Morris's wife. She just seemed to be the type that would never let go of anything once she had it."

"Yeah. You want to put on your robe, CJ?"

In the moment of the final takedown, CJ had forgotten she was naked. She covered herself with the robe that one of the detectives handed her. Hong simply stood staring at the motionless body on the floor until CJ was dressed again.

He looked at the blood running down CJ's arm and motioned for one of the squad officers to stop the bleeding.

"You better have that wound checked," Hong said matter-of-factly.

Blood was dropping on the floor from the slash across CJ's arm, and it suddenly began to hurt.

Rose came over and applied a dressing to stop the bleeding and then bandaged it up before they departed for the station with Amy Morris in tow.

CJ went to the bedroom and changed into jeans and blouse before leaving. She rode with Hong to the station before being sent to the hospital for stitches and a tetanus shot.

CJ found Rick at the hospital waiting for her. He came alone, not wanting to scare the children if it was something major. She fell into his arms and they kissed passionately before walking into the emergency room.

Back at the station, Hong had booked Amy Morris and released John and Diane from protective custody.

Amy had given a complete confession, relating every detail of every killing. Hong thought she was probably insane and he was almost certain she would spend the rest of her life in a mental institution. It was strange that during the confession she was calm and then would suddenly begin to rant and rave.

Hong left the interrogation room thinking that Amy Morris had a split personality, no doubt about it.

Hong sat down at his desk. It had been a wild case, filled with twists, turns, and blind alleys. Hong felt bad because he had not protected CJ to the best of his ability. The injury was minor, but still, it was an injury. The manila folders on the murders were sitting on his desk. He glanced through each one, looking at the photos and reading the data on each victim. Each was a wasted life; each victim was someone that had really done no wrong. Their lives had been ripped away, by events out of their control, but it was finally over. Hong looked up and closed the files slowly.

This case was closed.

The phone rang. He picked it up. It was the chief of police. There was another case for him and CJ on Maui and could they get on it by next Monday.

Hong told the chief about CJ's injury but said they should be able to be on assignment by Monday.

Hong hung up and leaned back in his chair.

"I wonder what CJ will say when I tell her we're going to Maui on Monday?" He shook his head.

No rest for the weary.

Printed in the United States
100811LV00007B/34/A